Blinded by his Love

Lock Down Publications and
Ca$h Presents
Blinded by his Love
A Novel by Destiny Skai

Blinded by his Love

Lock Down Publications
P.O. Box 870494
Mesquite, Tx 75187

Visit our website
www.lockdownpublications.com

Copyright 2018 by Blinded by his Love

First Edition October 2018
Printed in the United States of America

Lock Down Publications
Like our page on Facebook: Lock Down Publications @
www.facebook.com/lockdownpublications.ldp
Cover design and layout by: **Dynasty Cover Me**
Book interior design by: **Shawn Walker**
Edited by: **Kiera Northington**

Stay Connected with Us!

Text **LOCKDOWN** to 22828 to stay up-to-date with new releases, sneak peaks, contests and more…

Submission Guideline

Submit the first three chapters of your completed manuscript to
ldpsubmissions@gmail.com, subject line: Your book's title. The
manuscript must be in a .doc file and sent as an attachment.
Document should be in Times New Roman, double spaced and in
size 12 font. Also, provide your synopsis and full contact
information. If sending multiple submissions, they must each be in a
separate email.

Have a story but no way to send it electronically? You can still
submit to LDP/Ca$h Presents. Send in the first three chapters,
written or typed, of your completed manuscript to:

LDP: Submissions Dept
Po Box 870494
Mesquite, Tx 75187

DO NOT send original manuscript. Must be a duplicate.

Provide your synopsis and a cover letter containing your full contact
information.

Thanks for considering LDP and Ca$h Presents.

Destiny Skai

Acknowledgements

In honor of Domestic Violence month, I decided to write this story because it hits so close to home. Adult women are not the only victims in abusive relationships, teenagers are too, and I was a victim at the age of seventeen. Although this is a work of fiction, a lot of the things my character goes through are based upon my personal experiences, which is why many scenes are so detailed. Mental abuse is real and is far worse than physical. Your external scars will heal fast, but it takes years to heal psychological trauma.

Several times, I've had to pull away from this story because I became so emotional. And, after catching my breath and recuperating, I was finally able to finish. The best advice I can give is to talk to your daughters without judgement, recognize the signs, and share this story to let them know there is life after the abuse. If you know anyone that's going through abuse, tell them to get out now, or contact the National Abuse Hotline at 800-799-7233.

To all of my readers, thank you for following me throughout my writing journey and supporting my projects. It means the world to me and I know none of this would be possible without each and every last one of you. To my publishing family, LDP, thank you for your undying support and promoting my work. I appreciate all of you. Shawn Walker, I could write a book on the many ways you've assisted me throughout this journey, but I don't have to, because what's understood doesn't have to be explained.

And, last but not least, the CEO, Ca$h. Thank you for allowing me to release this story, because you know how important it was to me to get this story out. Your support has never wavered and you've always been my voice of reason and someone I could come to during my time of need. So many times

I've wanted to quit, but you always said you would never let that happen and I appreciate that. I couldn't have picked a better company to display my talent and for that, you have my LOYALTY.

To my family and close friends, I love y'all with everything in me and it's because of your love and undying support that I'm still writing. The way you support me is unbelievable. Whatever I sell, y'all buy. Even if it was a Popsicle stick with my name spelled out in rhinestones, y'all would buy it and I love y'all for that. My kids, Ethan and Torrence, everything I do is to benefit the both of you and one day, the fruits of my labor and legacy will belong to you too.

Prologue

My father had always taught me to know my self-worth, respect my body and never love anything or anyone that didn't love me back. And if a man couldn't do the things he did for me, I didn't need one. From the time I entered the sixth grade, he constantly drilled his words of wisdom into my brain. That was two years ago, and he continued to say the same thing.

"What's the number-one rule in life?"

"Never allow a man to strip me of my independence. Get my own money, so he can't control what I do and how I do it."

Pleased with my answer, he nodded his head and moved on to the next question. "And, what will happen if you give up your independence?"

"I forfeit my rights on having a voice and making my own decisions."

"What are you?"

"A princess."

"What will you never be to a man?"

"His bitch or ho."

"That's right and don't you forget it." He winked at me. "You're my number-one girl and I will always be by your side, no matter what. Anything you ever need in life daddy got you, baby."

"Can I ask you something?" I tilted my head to the side, because this question had been in my head for a while now.

"Shoot it."

"Do you wish I was a boy?"

At first he laughed, but when he saw that I was serious it ended abruptly. "No, sweetheart. I'm happy with you just the way you are. Now, I did want a son, so I could leave behind a legacy. But, since that didn't happen, I'm giving it all to you. Aniya doesn't act like me. She has your mother's traits, so I treat her differently. Nonetheless I love her, but she's not built like you."

The S-class Benz my father was pushing came to a complete stop in the driveway of a two-story pink house. It was dark outside, but I recognized it because it had a matching bird house in the front yard that I loved so much. I looked over at him as he picked up the car phone and dialed a number.

"I'm outside." I couldn't hear what was being said, so I just sat back and waited patiently for us to go home. Thank God we were only a few blocks away.

"I can't get out. I have my daughter with me," he replied before putting the phone back on the hook and getting out the car.

When I glanced up to check our surroundings, I saw the front door open and a man walk out carrying something in his hand. From my view they seemed to be exchanging a few words. Then, he handed my father whatever he was holding and walked away. I was curious about what he was doing and why we only came here at night, but I knew not to ask any questions. If it ever came down to that, my riding privileges would be terminated indefinitely. My father was a criminal defense attorney, so there was no telling what type of people he was defending.

As soon as he made it back to the car, he tossed the briefcase in the backseat and we were on our way.

"Are we going home now?" My brow furrowed and curiosity was all in my face.

After sitting through a long, yet boring awards ceremony for my academic achievements, my eyes couldn't take anymore.

My father always had this twinkle in his eye every time he looked at me. It made me feel special, knowing he was proud of me and that I was his number-one girl. Staring back at him was like looking in a mirror. We looked so much alike. Almost identical. We had the same caramel complexion, while Aniya took after our mother with her brown skin. That was part of the reason our bond was much stronger and the fact that I was his protégé.

We had a plan in place for me to attend his alma mater and become an attorney, just like him. All I wanted to do was walk in my father's footsteps and make him proud, but not my sister, she wanted to be a dance instructor. When she broke the news to him, he had a fit.

"Tell him honey," our mother insisted.
"Tell me what? Yo' ass better not be pregnant," he shouted.
Aniya didn't make direct contact with him. She kept her eyes on her plate. "I'm not going to Harvard and I don't want to be a lawyer. I want to be a dance instructor."
"Like hell you will and if you do, I'm not paying for that shit. Dance instructors don't make six figures, so I suggest that you get your priorities in order."

"Yes, princess, I am taking you home."

"Where are you going?" My eyes widened in surprise.

"I have some business to handle, but I promise I'll be back before you go to sleep."

"But it's already dark, can't you just stay please?" I couldn't let him go because I hated being in the house without him. Anxiety took over my young body and a terrible feeling came over me. Tears welled up in my eyes and cascaded slowly down my face. "I'm afraid you won't come back and I'll never see you again."

When he didn't reply right away, I fell into a sunken place. If anything was to happen to him, I swear I would die. Nobody on earth loved me as much as he did. He pulled into our driveway and to my surprise, he turned the car off. He sighed, then grabbed my hand. "I will never leave you and I want you to understand that, so stop crying."

"Mama said you cheating on her with another bitch," I confessed truthfully.

"What?" Several wrinkles surfaced on his forehead and that only happened whenever he became aggravated. "When did she say that?"

"Every time you run errands she says it and that's why you can't leave me here with her. She's mean to me when you're not around."

"Leilani, stop it. You don't have to say all of that to get me to stay home."

I could no longer contain my emotions, so I started to sob loudly. He needed to accept the truth, because lying to him wasn't tolerated in our home and I knew better than to do so. The taste of my salty snot hit my lips, but I didn't care. I was in pain and I needed to be heard. He had no clue about the treatment I was subjected to in his absence, underneath the roof he paid for.

"Daddy, I'm not lying, I swear. Every time you leave, she calls me names and says I'm no good, just like you."

My daddy closed his eyes and bit down on his lip. "Come on. Let me take you inside."

As we walked through the pathway of our ranch-style home, I caught a quick glance at the flower bed my father and I planted months ago. A sudden wave of nervousness came over me, causing my hands to tremble when we stepped onto the porch. He unlocked the door and pushed it open, so I could walk in first.

The family room was adjacent to the front door and that's where my mother was sitting, watching television. "We're back," he spoke loudly to get her attention.

"Great." Her voice was flat and she never took her eyes off her favorite show. In her hand was her drinking glass and that meant one thing. She was drunk.

I walked behind him as he approached her. The remote was sitting beside her, so he picked it up and powered it off. "Don't you want to see your daughter's certificates?"

"That could've waited until I was done." Her mouth was twisted up in utter disgust. Seeing her nonchalant reaction made me feel like she didn't care one way or another about my achievements. As a child, that hurt me to the depth of my soul.

"Are you drunk?" he asked.

Diane held her glass up then took a sip. "Maybe. Maybe not." Her head moved like it was on a swivel.

A few months back she had a car accident that left her in bad shape, so she was on all types of medication. My mother had become addicted to them over a course of time, claiming it was the only way she could cope. That was when the verbal abuse started. She refused treatment on more than one occasion, although she desperately needed it.

"When I get back, we are going to have a serious talk." My father kissed me on the forehead. "I'll be back, go upstairs and get ready for bed."

"Where are you going, Leonardo?" she asked.

"On an errand and don't worry, it's not another bitch, as you so eloquently put it."

We both walked off at the same time. "Leilani, come here."

The moment Diane called my name, my heart dropped to the pit of my stomach. In my eyes, she wasn't a mother to me, so I referred to her by her first name. I turned around and walked slowly to the couch. She waited until she heard the front door close.

"So, you've been talking to your no-good-ass daddy about me, huh?" My eyes were blinking constantly, but I didn't respond to her.

"You no-good, dirty little bitch. You gone be just like his ass when you grow up and I wish I never gave birth to you. I don't give a fuck how many certificates you bring in this house. I will never be proud of you. It's a waste of time. All you gone be in life in a useless whore, just wait and see."

Those words cut me to the core and shattered my heart, as they poured from the lips of the woman that was supposed to love me unconditionally. My bottom lip quivered and the tears from my eyes flowed heavily.

Diane drew her hand back and slapped me hard across the face. I screeched in pain, holding my cheek. She had never taken it this far by being physical and it scared me, so I attempted to run. My legs didn't move fast enough, because she grabbed me by my hair and slung me onto the floor.

"Stop!" I screamed from the top of my lungs.

Seconds later, I heard a voice boom through the room. "What the fuck you doing to my child?"

It was such a relief to hear my father's voice. He rushed over and snatched Diane off me, slinging her ass to the floor. Instead of helping me up, he stood over her with his hands around her throat, squeezing hard.

"That's how you talk to her when I'm not around?" I finally got up from the floor and walked closer to where they were. In all my thirteen years of living, I had never seen him so angry. He reminded me of a ferocious lion I saw on Animal Planet, protecting its cub. To some degree, it felt good to see him defend me, but he had always told me no man should ever hit a woman.

Diane was on the floor kicking and clawing, trying to break free from the tight grip he had on her. Her eyes were watery and red, but that wasn't enough to make him stop. As he glared down at her, his brown eyes had fire in them and his lip was curled tight.

"Bitch, you gave birth to her and you would treat her this way? God can mark my words right now, and you can store this in your memory bank." He lifted her by the base of her neck until their noses were close enough to touch. "If I ever catch you disrespecting or touching her again, I will kill you."

As much I as hated her at that moment, I didn't want him to kill her. I just wanted him to teach her a lesson and make her stop treating me so badly. I called out to him softly. "Daddy, stop please."

Our eyes met and he locked in on me for a few seconds. Suddenly, his hard, cold stare softened and he gently released Diane from his grip. She was on the floor crying and coughing violently, trying to catch her breath. His attention went back to her.

"Diane, listen to me and I want you to digest what I'm about to say to you. At this moment, you have one option. Let me take

14

you to rehab, so you can get yourself together. If not, I will file for divorce tomorrow morning and I will take Aniya away from you."

Diane's body was shaking uncontrollably, while sprawled out on the floor. The tears she shed had her face glistening with moisture. "I'm sorry," she cried. "I'm sorry."

My daddy stood up, walked over to me and held me in his arms. "I'm so sorry, Leilani. I wish you would've told me sooner. I had no idea this was going on, but I can promise you that it will never happen again."

"You let her take my place." Diane was sobbing loud and drooling out the mouth. "You supposed to be my husband and you let a child take my place."

Being that young in age, I didn't know how to feel. I didn't understand what she meant. "What's wrong with her?"

"Your mother is sick. I'm going to get her some help, but right now I need you to go upstairs."

"Okay."

The very next day, my father dropped her off to rehab where she remained for twelve months. During that time, I was forced to do visits, but our conversation was non-existent. Diane barely looked at me because she was too busy conversing with Aniya. Truthfully, I didn't care because I was used to that type of treatment. I just never understood why a mother could hate her daughter so much. Hell, it wasn't like she was my stepmom. It didn't matter to me anymore because while she was away, those were the best days of my life.

Destiny Skai

Chapter 1

Coy

"Fuck nigga, give it up." I kicked Reggie in the face with my olive-green Timberland boots. He was an older cat, but he deserved the ass kicking he was getting. Blood gushed from his mouth and his teeth hit the floor. My instincts caused me to jump backwards swiftly, to keep the bright red blood from ruining my fresh kicks.

"I oughta stomp your brain out yo' fuckin' head for getting that shit on my fresh-ass boots." I kicked him in the ribs like I was playing kick ball and he folded at the waist, holding his stomach.

"Come on, man. It ain't gotta be like this." Reggie moved aimlessly around the floor like the spineless snake he was. Any nigga that would set up his homie, after he helped him get on his feet, wasn't shit to be fucked up with and he needed to be bodied. Nowadays, you couldn't trust these niggas. They didn't know shit about loyalty and would throw their day-ones under the bus without blinking. But, that wasn't the only reason I was on his ass.

"I told you I was coming to collect, and you tried to play me. You gone try and get ghost like I wouldn't find you." I raised my foot and stepped on the side of his head.

"Arghh!" he shouted. "The bag," he heaved. "It's over there behind the couch. Just get it and let me go please."

I knelt with my gun in my hand and rubbed that shit across his temple and forehead, taunting him. "Nah, I ain't letting you go, old head. That's a negative."

"I just gave you what you asked for. Come on, man. You really want to go to prison for murder, for killing another brother? That's not what you want."

Reggie was doing his best to convince me not to squeeze that trigger, but his fate was decided five years ago. I made a promise to my father that I would handle this shit and I was standing firm on what I believed in and my promise.

"Brother?" I laughed, hawked up some spit and showered his face with it. "Nigga, you think I give a fuck about that brotherhood bullshit? Fuck no. You wasn't worried about that shit when you killed my black daddy."

"Your daddy? I don't know what you talking about and I don't know your daddy either." He continued to squirm on the floor.

"Oh yeah, you do, so stop all that muthafuckin' lyin' 'cause you pissing me off."

Reggie wiped his face with his shirt. "Man, I swear I don't know what you talking about."

Whap!

My gun crashed down on the side of his face a few more times. "Nigga, don't play on my intelligence." Sweat and blood spurted in the air, making a crash landing on my face, but I ignored it. "Let me refresh your memory."

The thought of my father hurt my heart. He loved me more than my own mother did, and I knew that was due to the nature of their relationship. They were together for a few years before I was born, and they were in love. That was, until I arrived. My father always knew he was going to be successful eventually and he wanted the same for my mom, but she had other plans. All she wanted to do was party and he wasn't having it. He gave her an ultimatum and when she didn't fall through with the plan, he left her for another woman.

When I was younger, I thought he just abandoned us, but then when I got older, it all came full circle the moment he explained everything to me. My father had big plans for my life, but that was cut short, thanks to the pig on the floor squealing.

"I didn't do nothing, man," he yelled.

"You came into my father's home and pretended to be a friend." The flashback of that night flashed into my mind and I could feel the tears welling up in my eyes. "All along, you was plotting and planning. I'll never forget that night. There was arguing. He told you that you could've gotten anything from him and you didn't need to rob him. You apologized and shot my daddy in the back of the head, as he tried to get the money out the drawer."

Reggie's eyes were consumed with guilt, as I forced him to revisit his heinous crime. "I'm sorry, man, but I was on drugs and I owed this dealer. He was going to kill me if I didn't come up with my money to pay my debt."

"Your apology doesn't mean to shit to me. You killed my daddy, three siblings and my step-mama. I would've been dead too, if I wasn't quick on my feet when I jumped out the second-floor window."

Reggie kept crying about how sorry he was, but I wasn't trying to hear that shit. I stayed by his side and watched snot bubbles and blood combine with one another and slide down to his lip. That shit was gross, but I had seen worse.

"Nigga, shut the fuck up." I stood up and took the Black & Mild from behind my ear and lit it. The whole ordeal was stressing me the fuck out, but after I witnessed him take his last breath, I knew for a fact I would feel better. To take the edge off, I took a few pulls and blew the smoke out my nose.

"Were you sorry when you blew my old boy brains out in front of his family?" As expected, he didn't mumble a single word. "No. Of course you weren't, so I don't want to hear none of that shit."

The Black & Mild hung from my lip, as I took a long drag from it. The bright red cherry bomb looked like a little ball of fire. I knelt down once more and mashed the black in his eye.

"Arrggghhh." He screamed to the top of his lungs, while shaking on the floor like he was having a seizure, and holding his eye.

"That shit don't feel good, huh?" With my fist clutched tight, I punched him in the face repeatedly, causing more damage to his bloody, swollen face.

"Well nigga, this the same type of pain I felt when I lost my ol' boy. You gone suffer before I kill you, I promise you that. I couldn't wait until I ran into your ass after all these years."

Whenever I did my dirt, I did it solo because I knew I wouldn't tell on myself. It was hard to beat a case with a witness or a co-defendant. Especially if that nigga wasn't solid and would fold easily under pressure. Nope. Not on my watch. Before I kidnapped the nigga and brought him to my uncle's studio, I went by the store and grabbed some shit that would burn. I walked over to the chair, pulled out my special ingredient and took the top off.

"Coy, what you doing? Come on, please, I had enough. I'll give you whatever you want."

"Can you bring my muthafuckin' ol' boy back? Nah, I didn't think so." I stood over him and poured the acid over his face and body.

"Ahhhhhhh."

The skin on his face and hands started to peel as soon as it made contact. I stood back and watched him buck on the floor, while trying to wipe his face. That only made it worse because the skin was sliding off as he wiped the fluid away. After I grew tired of listening to his horrific screams, I placed two bullets in his face.

Pow! *Pow*! Justice served.

Chapter 2

Leilani

Happy birthday to me. I couldn't believe I was finally eighteen. The legal age limit to do whatever I wanted to do. I swear it took me forever to get to the highlight of my life. High school was about to be behind me, then I was on my way to attend Harvard University, just like my father. My future was looking mighty bright.

There was a special man in my life and he meant the world to me. He was everything a girl could ask for and more. For the past seven months, we have been in sheer bliss. At first, my father was reluctant about us dating, but Coy remained persistent until he received his approval to take me out. His undying attempts were over the top at times, but he never gave up. It took sixty-six days of sending me one single rose daily, teddy bears and greeting cards. He even went as far as sending dinner cuisines from restaurants, with special desserts. We had never seen anything like it. On the sixty-sixth day, we received dinner from a soul food joint we were dying to try. That was the day my father reached out to Coy and invited him over to join us for dinner. After that, the rest was history.

Tonight, Coy was taking me out to celebrate my freedom and I was ecstatic. I had no clue about where we were going, but to be on the safe side, I opted to wear a dress. At least this way, I was prepared to go anywhere. After applying some lip gloss, I grabbed my clutch and a pair of back-up slides, just in case we had to walk.

On my way downstairs, the sound of the doorbell echoed throughout the house. My father opened the door and in walked Coy. He was dressed down in Polo, looking all spicy for me. My man was fine with his chocolate ass.

"Good evening, Mr. Jordan." He and my father shook hands.

"How you doing, Coy?"

"I'm good. No complaints over here."

"Did you look into what we talked about?"

Coy nodded his head and rubbed his hands together. "Yes sir, I did. I'm meeting up with him on Monday so I can get started."

"That's very good. Investing is important and very lucrative. You wanna be able to provide for your family and make sure they never see you struggle. That's what a provider does."

"Understood and thank you."

"As long as you with my daughter, I will always guide you down the right path."

I cleared my throat. "Excuse me, but I'm standing here."

"And you looking lovely doing that baby, but I was talking to the head of the household." Coy laughed and so did my father.

"Not funny." I pouted.

"Stop being a baby. Aren't you an adult now?" Coy joked.

"Yep, but it's my daddy fault I'm like this."

My daddy held his hands up. "Hey, I was only doing my job, but y'all go ahead and get out of here." He walked up and kissed me on the cheek. "Be safe and I'll see you later."

"We will," I answered.

"Take care of my baby, man. I'm leaving her in your hands."

They shook hands for the last time.

"I got her, Mr. J, don't worry." Coy smiled, then grabbed my hand and escorted me outside.

"Damn baby, you look good as hell in that dress." He put his fist over his mouth. "I was trying so hard not stare in front of yo' daddy."

"Oh really." I was blushing hard as hell. "I don't know why. You could've looked."

"Not in front of him." He opened the passenger door and waited until I was inside to close it.

Coy walked to the driver's side and got in. I sat my clutch on the side of me and got comfortable for the ride. I was so anxious to see where we were going. After he started the car, he changed the CD, then we were on our way.

The sound of a piano came through the speakers and the song immediately caught my attention. It was Jesse Powell's "You." That particular melody had become our favorite song. It displayed the way we felt about one another. I scooted to the middle of the seat and grabbed his hand, intertwining our fingers. Out of the list of qualities a man should have, Coy had them all. I felt safe when I was with him and loved when he held me in his arms. I laid my head on his arm and closed my eyes, thinking about the wedding I hoped to plan with him one day, while this song played in the background.

The way you walk, the way you talk
The way you say my name and smile
The way you move me, the way you soothe me
The way you speak softly through the night
Every morning you rise and open your eyes
I just wanna be there with you baby
I just wanna be yours, from this day forth

The movement of the car stopped and I felt Coy move his hand. "Baby, get up."

"I wasn't sleep." When I sat up, we were in the parking lot of a hotel. "What are we doing here?"

"I had to slide up on my homeboy and get some weed. We won't be here long, I promise."

"I hope not." It was my birthday and I was ready to enjoy it with him and not his friend. I don't know why he couldn't get that before he picked me up.

He pointed towards the highway. "The beach right over there."

"Okay."

We held hands and walked through the parking lot until we reached the stairs. The area we were in was not familiar to me, but I knew he wouldn't just take me any place and jeopardize my safety. At the second flight of stairs, we walked down the hallway, passing a few doors and stopped.

"Hold on for a second." He reached into his pocket, but I didn't see what he pulled out. I was too busy looking around. "Come on."

I walked inside and the room was extremely dark. I tried to reach for an object to hold, but I didn't feel a thing. The only light we had was from the outside. Coy placed his hands on my waist and ushered me in once he closed the door.

"I can't see and I don't want to fall."

"I'm not gone let you fall. Just be still so I can turn on the light." Once he let me go, I stood in place like a statue.

"Happy birthday, baby." Red lights shined in the room and my mouth instantly dropped to the floor.

I couldn't believe what I was seeing. "Oh my God! Coy, this for me?" I shouted in excitement.

"Yes."

Immediately I started to fan myself to keep from crying tears of joy. "Don't cry. This is your day." I told myself.

He laughed at my dramatics. "It's okay, you can cry if you want to."

I shed a few tears, but I didn't allow it to go overboard. This was a special moment for me. "I'm just so happy right now. No one outside of my dad ever did anything this nice for me."

The room was decorated with several vases full of red, long-stemmed roses. Against the wall was a heart-shaped bed covered with rose petals, with a gold box sitting in the middle. On the floor, there was a plethora of shopping bags from Foot Locker and Macy's.

"You deserve all of this and I'm glad I was able to do this for you." Coy walked over to me and squatted down at my feet. One by one, he removed my heels. "I have something I want to give you."

"Haven't you given me enough?" I didn't care about material things, because Leonard Jordan was my father. Anything I thought I wanted, he would buy it. Just being with Coy was more than enough for me.

He leaned over and grabbed the box removing a diamond ring. Suddenly, my palms began to sweat and my heart rate increased. In my mind, all I was thinking about was a proposal. *Is this really happening to me? Did I really find my one true love?* A million questions flooded my mind at one time causing me to tremble.

Then, he burst my bubble. "I want you to wear this promise ring as a symbol of my love. This is to show you I will always love and take care of you. Will you wear it?"

"Yes." It wasn't the proposal I was looking for, but it was just as good.

Coy slipped the ring on my finger, then kissed my hand. "Don't ever take this off, okay? Them college dudes need to know you taken."

"I won't," I promised.

He pecked me on my lips. "I have one more surprise for you."

"I don't need anything else, baby." I placed the palm of my hand on his chest. "The only thing I want from you is the thing that's beating right now inside your chest cavity."

Standing face-to-face, I locked in on his big, brown dreamy eyes. "You already got that." I could've melted off those words alone. "Last thing, I promise."

Hand in hand, we walked over to the table and awaiting us was one large silver platter and a bottle of champagne on ice. "I didn't even see this." I giggled.

"Yeah, 'cause you walked in and looked one way." He pulled out my chair. "Have a seat, birthday girl." Coy removed the top of the platter and the strong, delicious smell of crab legs, lobster, shrimp and garlic potatoes filled my nose.

"This smells so good and I'm starving." I picked up the napkin close to my right hand and placed it on my lap. It was time to dig in, but he was too busy fixing drinks. "What is that?"

"Dom Perignon."

"Is that liquor?"

"Champagne." I took the wine glass he handed to me. "Drink up, baby. It's your night."

After dinner, I was full and buzzed from the drinks I consumed. Coy was sitting on the dresser smoking his blunt and rocking to the music. He looked over at me with those sleepy Chinese eyes and giggled. "You good over there?"

"Yeah."

"Come hit this." He held the blunt out.

"Baby, you know I don't smoke."

"Please. Just hit it one time for your birthday." If he grinned any harder, I was certain his cheeks would've gotten stuck.

Since it was my birthday, I decided to go ahead and have my first experience with the one I loved. "How do I smoke it?"

"Give it back so I can show you." Coy took a toke of the weed and inhaled it. Some came out his nose and the rest was from his mouth. "Pull it slow. If you do it too hard, you gone choke."

I took the first pull and did exactly what he showed me and damn near killed myself with all that coughing. He was killing himself laughing. "You laughing just a little too hard."

"I told you don't pull it like that."

"Okay I'll try again." This time it was smoother and once I was comfortable, the blunt disappeared and I was higher than a giraffe's ass. I could barely keep my eyes open. My rookie ass was super light-headed, but I felt good though. Although, my head felt like it would roll off my neck at any moment.

"Baby, you high?" His eyes got even lower when he giggled.

"That's what it's called?" I giggled right along with him. "Cause if it is, then yes."

"Come here." I walked over and stood in between his legs.

Coy had this seductive look in his eyes, as he bit down on his bottom lip. That shit was so sexy to me. The cool temperature from his hand sent chills down my spine, when he placed it on the back of my neck, pulling me close to him.

Our lips connected and we were engaged in a deep, intoxicating kiss. That alone was damn near erotic. I could feel his hand exploring my body slowly, like he had just discovered new land. His touch alone had me weak in the knees, so I placed my hand on his thigh. Coy moved his hand from my neck, grabbed my hand and placed it between his legs. My heart stopped beating for a few seconds when I felt the size of his penis. It was hard and thick, so I drew my hand back fast. That put fear in my heart and I wasn't sure if I wanted to proceed.

Coy stopped our kiss, but he didn't move his lips from mine. "What's wrong?"

"Nothing," I lied.

"You scared?"

I swallowed hard and blinked a few times before I answered, "No." That was lie number two in less than one minute.

My inner person screamed, *yes bitch, we are scared. Yo' ass still a virgin.*

"Back up." Coy jumped from the dresser and placed his hands on my waist, pushing me towards the bed.

When he kissed me again, it was more intense. He grabbed the bottom of my dress and tugged on it. "Take this off."

I was nervous like a hooker standing in front of a whole congregation. My hands were even shaking when I pulled the dress over my head. I dropped it to the floor and stood there in my bra and panties. His eyes roamed my body hungrily like he wanted to eat me alive.

"Damn, my baby fine. You gone make me fuck a nigga up." I could barely laugh. My nerves were too damn shot. "Take that off too and relax." He went towards the table while I continued to undress.

Once I was naked, I climbed onto the bed and laid down on my back, with my arms covering my small perky titties. When he returned, he was holding a full glass of champagne. "Down this so you can loosen up."

I sat up and killed the whole glass with no problem and handed it back to him. "Good girl." He smiled, while removing his clothing.

The waiting game was long, as I sat with anticipation for him to come out his boxers. I needed to get a good look at what I was about to get myself into. When he pulled them down, I cringed. His penis was a lighter brown than his actual complexion and it had veins on it. My eyes widened at the sight. It was pretty and evenly toned, but I didn't know how I planned on taking all of that. To keep from torturing myself, I laid back down and focused on everything except Coy. I was amused at the sight of the mirror on the ceiling. I didn't notice that either when I walked in.

Coy climbed in between my legs and glared down at me. "You sure you wanna do this?"

"I'm sure." Coy was my man and I wanted him to be my first and only.

Chapter 3

Leilani

As soon as I gave him the green light, he laid flat on his stomach, pushed my legs apart and buried his head in between my thighs. The moment his lips grazed my lower region, my body tensed up. He placed soft kisses on my inner thighs, teasing me. His warm, wet tongue slid up and down my center rapidly.

"Mm."

Coy put his mouth on my vagina and tongue kissed her the same way he did my other set of lips. That shit drove me wild. I found myself rocking my hips and getting into it. He sucked harder and harder, like he was trying to suck my soul out my body.

"Mm." His tongue gained entrance to my opening and I could feel it slither in and out of the crease. Biting down on my clit, he nibbled on it gently with his teeth. "Ss. Mm. Oh my God," I cried out.

My quick reflexes caused my legs to clamp themselves shut, locking down on his head. Coy rose to his knees, then placed both of his hands on my knees and pushed them up to my stomach. Head first, he shoved his tongue back inside and slurped up my juices. My legs started to shake and I could no longer keep them still.

"Ah. Ah."

I squirmed, trying to get away from his lethal tongue. That thang had me about to climb the wall. My body managed to get away from him, so he grabbed my legs and pulled me back to him.

"Stop running."

He wiped my juices from his lips and climbed on top of me. That thang was hard as a rock. The veins were thick like the lines on a Snickers bar. It was sticking straight out, pressing hard against my lips.

"We should use a condom." Sure enough, I was inexperienced, but I knew the consequences of unprotected sex and my daddy wasn't having that.

"I trust you. Don't you trust me?"

"You know what I mean. My daddy would kill me." I trusted him, I just didn't trust the fact that I wouldn't get pregnant during my first sexual encounter.

He leaned down and kissed me in the mouth. "I promise not to get you pregnant. I'll pull out."

"No. I'm scared." I was not trying to put myself at risk like that. College was months away and I couldn't afford to have any accidents. My father would have both of our heads on a platter.

"Trust me, baby. I'm not ready for kids either."

I was agreeing to something I knew nothing about, but I was praying that he knew what he was doing, because I sure as hell didn't.

We engaged in a little more foreplay to keep me sexually aroused. Coy was a multi-tasker. He sucked and licked on my neck, while rubbing my kitty to get her extra wet. I could feel the tip of his fat head pressing against me, but it wouldn't go in. I was too tight for him to just slide in, so he backed up and inserted one finger, then a second one to make it expand. My juices and his finger action started making squishy sounds.

"Yeah, she ready."

My scary ass closed my eyes quick, like that was going to help. Coy tapped his dick against my lips, then pushed past my delicate flaps, to gain full access to my virgin tunnel. Thrusting against my pelvis, he broke his way through my tough barrier, tearing my hymen. My back arched to the max and a loud piercing scream filled the room and bounced around the walls like an echo.

Coy covered my face with tender kisses, while long-stroking me slowly. "You okay?"

"It hurts."

Tears filled my eyes and I could no longer see a clear image of his face. Gently, he wiped away the water with his hand. My petite frame rocked along with his muscular body, making what some would call beautiful music. I wasn't there yet, because every stroke felt like my walls were being stretched and ripped apart. So, in my mind, all I heard was Freddy Kruger music. My breathing pattern was all out of whack. I was skipping beats and getting air trapped in my throat.

"Ow. Ow. Ow." My bottom lip quivered. My hands desperately searched for something to hold on to, but there was nothing there besides the sheets. So, I gripped those and squeezed them tight.

"You want me to stop?"

"No." I did, but I didn't want him to see me as a little girl. All I wanted was for the pain to subside. I lifted my legs and I could feel something warm run down my thigh. It felt sticky when his pelvis touched mine. I ignored it and locked my legs onto his. My pussy muscles had his dick gripped tight causing heavy friction down there. The sheets weren't helping at all. I needed something else to grab and his body was my only option. His head was buried deep into my neck, sucking on my hot spot and playing with my erect nipples.

Coy pushed into me slowly and his rod went deeper, sinking into corners I didn't know existed until now. The deeper he went, the further my nails sunk into his back.

"Ahh. Baby. Coy. Please." My words were all gibberish.

My eyes zoomed in on the mirror mounted against the ceiling. Being able to see him move and grind on top of my body was something I couldn't explain. It took me to a different place, my early teenage years, which allowed me to forget about the pain for a little while.

"Let's make a pact, Leilani, that we will lose our virginity together," Caussia suggested, while we were sitting on the front porch engaging in girl talk.

"I don't know how that's going to play out, but we can try." We picked up our soda cans, clinked them together and took a

sip. "And for the record, whoever I lose my virginity to we are getting married."

And I still felt that way.

The sound of our skin slapping erupted and brought me back to reality when he drilled me without warning. I tried holding onto him tight in an effort to slow him down, but that didn't work. He kept on pounding away at my box. My insides felt like they were in fire.

"Ow! Ow! Slow down." It sounded like I was yodeling. Right away, he slowed down and handled my body, just the way I wanted him to. After a while the shot of champagne took effect, easing the pain just a little. So, it didn't hurt too badly.

"I wanna hold you," he whispered.

That blew me because I didn't know what he was talking about. "What you mean?"

"I'll show you, get up."

Coy got up, sat on the edge of the bed and planted his feet on the floor. "Come sit in my lap."

In my heart I wasn't ready to try new positions, but I also couldn't turn him down even though my pussy was aching. Just when I was about to straddle him, I caught a glimpse of some blood between his legs and mine, so I paused in front of him.

"Don't worry about it, that's natural." He was trying to school me. After all, he had more experience than I did.

I took his word for it and eased down onto his dick slowly. My walls stretched slowly and adjusted to the thickness of the base, filling me up and fitting him tight like a glove. It wasn't all the way in, so with a little assistance, Coy slipped his arms underneath mine, bringing his hands on my shoulders and pulled me down forcibly onto him. I yelped out in pain.

"Ahhh. That hurts."

"Just relax and wrap your legs around my waist." I did as I was told, even though it was uncomfortable, and let Coy take control of what was to happen next.

As promised, he held me tight and rocked my body on top of his at a steady pace. We remained upright on the edge of the bed as our bodies grinded back and forth on one accord. After a few minutes of being extra, I was finally able to relax, and we were able to make some beautiful music.

My lips grazed his in the midst of me panting, our tongues interlocked, and things grew intense quickly. I kissed him harder and sucked his tongue, all while caressing his body. The sound of Kut Klose's "I Like" played softly in the background.

Tender lovin', is what I want
Don't want to rush it, nah
Let's take it nice n slow, honey
Caress my body, and hold me tight
Don't let me go, baby until I get enough
Baby tonight (baby tonight)
The lovin' is right
You know how I like it
You know how I want it

Everything about the sex was sensual. I didn't feel rushed and he took his time with my body and made sure I was satisfied. My neck was going to have so many hickies, for sure, because he couldn't keep his mouth and tongue off my body. There was no hiding that.

"Ooh. Mm. Mm," I moaned. "I love you so much." A lone tear escaped my eye the minute I said those words.

"I love you too, baby."

My insides started to contract and vibrate, while I rode him with guidance. I didn't know what was happening, but I wasn't about to stop it. This experience had me feeling shit I never felt before. After a few more strokes, I couldn't hold it any longer. "I have to pee," I moaned in his ear.

"That's not pee. You about to nut and so am I." Coy gripped my booty cheeks, forcing me to bounce up and down on his dick.

"I can feel it. Don't hold it?"

"Nah, cream all over this dick." The banging was harder and harder, so I bit down on his neck to take my mind off of my own pain. He had my pussy in flames and I wanted to scream, but I was having mixed emotions. It hurt, but at the same time it felt good. There was an eruption inside of me and my soul began to cry, flooding him with vaginal tears. That was an experience I definitely wanted to feel again.

Coy started to breath hard. "Shit. Shit. Ooh. Fuck." He grunted. The noises continued for another minute. "Ooh, I'm finna nut in this pussy. Shit." I was caught up in the moment that I ignored the words that came from his mouth. "I'm puttin' a baby in yo' ass."

The grip he had on my shoulders became tighter with every thrust. "You gon' have my baby?"

"I can't," I whimpered into his ear.

"That's the wrong answer." Coy raised up with me in his arms and laid me down on my back with his dick still in me. He raised my leg, leaned in close to my body and dug deep into my pussy, causing me to scream.

"Ouuu," I shouted like I was catching the Holy Ghost. "Coy, it hurts."

"I ain't stopping until you say it."

The power of the stroke had me saying anything. He was killing me, and I couldn't hold out any longer. I needed a break and some water, so I gave up.

"Okay. Okay," I cried.

"Okay what?" he grunted.

"I'll have your baby." I didn't mean it, I just wanted him to stop.

Coy's body jerked a few times, as he sunk deeper and deeper into my walls. He was completely drenched in sweat. "I'm coming for real this time. Be still."

I just laid there and waited on him to finish and when he was done, he laid down beside me.

"Damn, you gone have a nigga sprung." I moved closer to him and laid my head on his chest, while we took a few moments to catch our breath.

"Me too," I agreed.

***

The next day I was exhausted and physically drained. We had sex so many times and in so many positions, I lost count. I swear I didn't get a wink of sleep. Every time I dozed off, it didn't last very long, 'cause he was constantly digging up in me. The very last time was about two hours ago, right before check-out time at noon. All I could do was lay there like a dead fish. My limbs were sore and so was my nookie. This was brand-new to us, because I never masturbated or inserted anything inside of me. Obviously, there's a first time for everything.

When we pulled up in the driveway, my father's car was there. I didn't expect him to be home on a Saturday afternoon before three o'clock. Fooled my ass. So now, my mind was racing and wondering if he was waiting on me to see when I would arrive, since he couldn't get in contact with me. This was my first time ever staying out overnight with Coy, therefore I wasn't sure what to expect when I walked through that door. Since I was eighteen, that should count for something.

The car was still running, so I turned my attention to Coy. "You not getting out?" I couldn't lie I was a little nervous.

"You want me to?"

"Yes. I don't know what he's going to say when I get in there. You know I never stayed out overnight under any circumstances."

"I think you being paranoid, but I'll get out and talk to him."

"Thank you." That made me feel better, knowing that I didn't have to face the music alone.

"Give me a kiss before we go in."

I leaned over and tongued him down like I wasn't going to see him again. My body shivered the moment his hand touched my face and moisture between my legs made an appearance, so I pulled back.

"That's enough." I was ready to go inside and get this over with. It wasn't like he could put me on punishment. *Hell, I was grown!*

When I walked through the door, I dropped my keys inside the Denny's bag I was carrying. The sound of the television caught my attention, so we headed in that direction until we were standing directly beside him.

"Hi, Daddy." I smiled, trying to win him over before it even started.

"Good afternoon, Mr. J."

My father looked at both of us in silence. His facial expression was like blah, so I couldn't tell what type of mood he was in. When he got ready to say something, he took a deep breath. "You two have a seat."

Coy and I sat across from him on the other sofa. I placed my hands in my lap and waited anxiously on what he was about to say.

"So, how was your night?" His focus was on me, so I answered promptly.

"It was good."

"What did y'all do?"

Oh shit! I panicked. *Calm down, girl*, my inner self screamed, so I took a deep breath. "We went on the beach and had dinner."

He nodded his head up and down. "That's it?"

"Yes."

"Okay." His eyes shifted in Coy's direction, but I was still on his radar. "I want to explain something to the both of you. I understand that you've been an adult for..." he paused, then looked down at his Rolex watch. "For about thirty-eight hours now, but what I'm not going to tolerate is you staying out overnight, and gracing me with your presence well into the afternoon."

"Daddy," I whined, but he cut me off quick.

"I'm not finished. Do you know that I've been up since three o'clock this morning, wondering if the both of you were safe or not?" He held up one finger. "Or if something happened to the both of you?" He leaned back and crossed his legs.

"I've been sitting in this same spot for hours, just waiting on the police to show up at my door, or call me over the phone to deliver some bad news."

"Daddy, I'm sorry," I cried.

"Mr. Jordan, I apologize. That's my fault. I should've made sure that we called you. So, don't take it out on her please."

"You know, Coy, I like you. I think you are a very respectable young man and I truly believe you love my daughter, without a doubt. It takes a real man to apologize when he's in the wrong and I commend you for that."

"Thank you, sir, and you're right. I do love your daughter very much. I want to spend the rest of my life with her." Coy reached out and held my hand when he heard me sniffling. "Stop crying."

My father tilted his head a little and squinted his eyes in my direction, but he wasn't looking in my eyes. His focus was a lot lower. Before saying what was on his mind, he stroked the bottom of his chin. "Leilani, what is that on your finger?"

"Huh?"

"Your left hand. What is that?"

Coy and I looked down at my hand and replied in unison. "It's a promise ring."

"That's all it better be." This time he directed all of his attention on Coy. "I've already had one daughter skip town and run off to get married. I don't need another one doing the same thing."

"You don't have to worry about that. I would never disrespect you on that level and ruin the friendship we've built over these last seven months. Leilani and I had a discussion about the meaning behind the ring. It represents a token of my love and commitment to her while she's away at college. When the time is right I will come to you and ask for her hand in marriage."

For the first time, my father actually smiled. "I like that. I like that a lot." Then, he rose to his feet and walked over to Coy and shook his hand. "You are a fine young man and when that time comes, I will gladly give you my daughter's hand. You remind me of myself when I was your age."

"Thank you, sir. I appreciate the comparison to a man of your caliber and that's the truth."

I was relieved that we could all sit and have a conversation like adults.

My father stuck his hands down in his pockets and took a step away from us. "Now that we have that squared away let's address the elephant in the room."

Oh Lord! Here we go.

"Are the two of you having sex?"

"No," I blurted out quickly.

I swear this man didn't waste no time getting to straight to the point, but I tried my best not to sweat and wear my guilt on my sleeve. I didn't want to lie to him, but I didn't want to tell him the truth either. This was definitely not a conversation I wanted to have with him. Not now, not later, or ever for that matter.

"Leilani, you've never lied to me in your life. So, don't start doing it now," he calmly stated.

"We are not having sex."

"Coy." He stopped before he could finish his sentence. "You know what? I'm not going to put you on the spot like that. I was a young man before, so I know what time it is."

This was the most uncomfortable conversation we've had since I've been on the planet. I'd rather run down I-95 butt naked during rush hour traffic, than to blatantly admit that Daddy's princess was no longer a virgin. *Nope!* I couldn't do it, so he might as well stop asking.

"Leilani, do you want to change your answer?"

"No."

"Okay, that's fine." He paced the floor for a few seconds before coming to a complete stop. Then, he folded his arms across his chest and looked at me with so much conviction, like he could see through my lie.

"I know for a fact that you're having sex and I'm going to tell you how I know that. The first thing I noticed when you walked in is the sudden change in your walk. The second thing I noticed is the plethora of passion marks on your neck."

Unconsciously, I brought my hand to my neck to see if there was any concrete evidence. I was busted and there was no way out of it. Growing up, he always used his courtroom tactics at home whenever he felt like deception was present and I should've known better than to think I could pull the wool over his eyes. He paid attention to everything.

"Lastly, when I asked what you did last night, you tensed up immediately."

"Okay, okay. I give up. Stop interrogating me like I'm a criminal on the stand," I shouted, while covering my face with my hands. "We had sex last night, but that was the first time I swear."

"Leilani, you're an adult now, so I can't monitor your movements or the things you do. But, I pray to God you were responsible enough to use condoms and if not, I strongly suggest you invest in birth control. I'm telling you right here and right now in front of him, so there's no confusion. Don't bring no baby home and that's all I have to say. Now, have a good day."

My father remained calm as he politely strolled out the room and went upstairs. I understood his point loud and clear without him having to yell once.

Chapter 4

Coy

Time had flown by quickly and our relationship had grown stronger than ever. Leilani had less than three weeks before she went off to college, so we spent all of our time together creating memories. After that situation with her father, we remained cool and he admitted he wasn't mad, just disappointed in our decision to take that next step in our relationship, without talking to him first. Then, he went on to say I would understand when I had a daughter of my own. I couldn't blame him for his reaction. No man wanted to picture Daddy's little girl with her legs open, getting dicked down by a nigga, while screaming his name. Mr. Jordan would probably want to kill me if he saw how I'd just had Leilani's legs pinned to the headboard, crying and calling on God.

"Baby," Leilani purred, while she was laid across my chest tracing imaginary circles around my nipple. "Are you sleeping?"

"Nah. What's up?" I cleared my throat.

"Are you still riding with my dad when he takes me to school?"

"No doubt. I wouldn't miss that for the world."

"Good." She sighed heavily. "I'm going to miss you so much while I'm away. You'll be down here enjoying yourself and I'll be up there suffering from separation anxiety."

"I'm only two hours and forty-six minutes away from you by plane and twenty hours by car. I'm never too far away to get to you. So, don't be surprised when I slide up on you unannounced."

"I see you did your homework." She sucked her teeth. "But, we shall see about that."

"Dead ass. You better believe that like you believe in ya' father's Holy Bible. And you better not be hugged up or giving my pussy away, 'cause I'll body you and that nigga."

That shit came out in a joking manner, but I meant every word I said from the heart and if she didn't know that, she better ask about me. My name was heavy in the streets and I ain't play no games.

"Well, you don't have to worry about that 'cause you my first and only, and there is nobody else in the world I would rather be with than you. I know you probably won't believe me, but I fell in love with you the moment we met. I used to dream about you all the time and wonder what it would be like to be with you. Now I know and I'll never let you go. I will love you unconditionally until the end of time."

Damn! That shit touched a nigga heart when she said that. I felt that deep down in my soul. Now she had me in my feelings like a bitch about to cry and shit, but I was too gangster to shed tears and expose my weakness. If she knew I was weak for her, she would probably try to play a nigga and use it to her advantage.

"That was deep and I know you love a nigga without you saying it. Your actions speak volumes, so I never doubted you. Just know that I love you too and I cherish the ground you walk on. You don't know this about me, but all this is new to me."

Leilani lifted her head and gazed at me with those beautiful brown eyes that hypnotized me, every time I looked in them for too long. "You've never been in love?"

"Sadly, no, I haven't. I've never loved any woman in my life."

"What about your mom?"

"Nah. I didn't love her either and honestly I think she felt the same way about me."

"I'm sorry, baby."

"You don't have to apologize, that was a long time ago and I'm over that."

Leilani eased back onto my chest and hugged me like she never wanted to let me go. Truth be told, I didn't want to let her go either. We both closed our eyes and slept until the late afternoon.

***

It was 5:32 p.m. when I woke up to the irritating sound of my cellphone. I swiveled my head in all directions looking for it, but it wasn't visible. Then finally, it dawned on me that it was in my pants pocket on the floor. That morning when I picked up Leilani, we came straight to my bedroom and stripped out of our clothes. The condom wrappers scattered across the floor was the proof that we had a busy day. I hated using them, but I promised her daddy we would and I was a man of my word.

Leilani's ass was knocked the fuck out. I had her ass snoring and salivating out the mouth. I was the *vagina slayer* in this bitch. Slowly pushing her to the side, I eased out the bed to see who the fuck was blowing me up. I picked up my gym shorts and pulled out my device.

"The one person I don't want to talk to," I mumbled and put it back inside my shorts.

Quickly and quietly, I picked up the wrappers from the floor, so I could take them to the trash. All five of them. Suddenly there was a knock on the door and I was confused because I didn't have company. The only person that came here on a regular basis was Sleeping Beauty over there.

Boom! Boom! Boom!

Whoever it was had a purpose and was determined to get in. I slipped on my shorts in a hurry, so I could see who I needed to drop. It was obvious they had guerilla nuts, trying me like that. On my way out the room, I grabbed my pistol from its hiding place and cocked it back. I looked through the peephole, but I couldn't see anybody.

Boom! Boom! Boom!

I removed the locks from the door and placed my hand on the knob. Locked and loaded, I put my finger on the trigger. I was ready to blast at any intruder, so I snatched the door open and aimed my gun at my target.

"Get that shit out my face, fool," Crystal snapped, pushing my hand out the way.

I dropped my hand since she wasn't a threat. The bitch was crazy though. "What the fuck you doing here?" I responded low, so I wouldn't wake up Leilani.

She put her hands on her hips. "I been texting you for the longest. Why didn't you call me back?"

"Man, get the fuck outta here with that. I don't have to answer when you call or text me."

Crystal tried to maneuver her way inside, but I blocked the entrance. "Who the fuck you got in here?"

"None of your business. We ain't together." I wanted to shut the door so bad, but I knew she wouldn't stop banging on the door.

"You wasn't saying none of this when you wanted some pussy two months ago."

I bit down on my lip and took a deep breath. "Check it. I'm trying real hard to keep from goin' in yo' shit, but you skatin' on thin muthafuckin' ice."

"Fuck you," she screamed. "I ain't goin' nowhere, so you might as well wake the bitch up, 'cause I know she in there." She rocked side to side with each syllable.

Instead of arguing with her, I pushed the door closed, but she kicked it and it flew back open on my foot. At that point, all I saw was red and a disrespectful bitch that didn't know her place. She tried me for the last time, so I punched her ass right in her dick suckers. I tried to knock that bitch teeth down her throat. That'll teach her about getting slick with me.

Crystal screamed as blood leaked from her mouth. She grabbed her shirt and wiped her mouth. "I'm a send the police right over here, watch."

I wasn't worried about her doing shit, because we fought damn near every day when we were together, so I had to leave her alone. I hated a hardheaded broad. She was one of those females that didn't feel loved unless her nigga was beating her ass, so a lot of the times she did shit to provoke the ass whoopings.

"Baby, what's going on?" The sound of Leilani's soft voice coming from behind me made my heart drop to the pit of my stomach. *Fuck!* This was not going to end well.

When I turned around to face her, she was standing there in her bra and a pair of my boxers with her arms folded across her chest. "Baby please, just give me a minute and I'll explain everything to you. I promise. Take this." I handed her my pistol and kissed her on the forehead.

"So you gone stand here and call another bitch 'baby' and kiss her in front of me?" Crystal screamed.

When I turned around to face Crystal, she was walking towards me, so I mushed her. "Bitch, we not together and I wish you get that shit through yo' fuckin' skull." I made sure I was close to her, just in case she couldn't hear me. "I don't want you. What we had is over. I moved on and you need to do the same thing. This is who I'm with."

"That's not what you was saying two months ago when you was fuckin' me."

"Bye, man. Get the fuck on befo' I beat yo' ass for real."

Leilani was quiet the whole time, until she heard that. "Hold on, what did you just say?" She stepped closer to where we were standing.

"We fucked two months ago."

"Coy, is that true?"

That shit had me heated. I couldn't lie to her, 'cause I was already busted. "I can explain."

Leilani was looking at me like she wanted to kill me. Those sparkling brown eyes I loved so much seemed darker, yet glassy. I hurt her and now I was about to pay for it. "You can leave now. Thanks for letting me know my man fucked you."

Crystal sized my baby up and down and rolled her neck. "Bitch, I'm not..."

That was the last word to leave her mouth. Leilani kicked that bitch in the stomach and caught her ass with a two-piece. Crystal stumbled backwards over the threshold and hit the floor. I sat back and watched Leilani stand over her and punch her repeatedly in the face. After watching for a while, I realized that Crystal wasn't gone get up on her own. I grabbed Leilani by the waist and lifted her midair. On the way up, she managed to sneak in one last kick.

"Call me a bitch again, dumb ass ho'." Crystal ole messy ass was getting off the floor as me and Leilani was going inside. That's what she get for poppin' up to my shit unannounced.

As soon as I placed Leilani down on her feet she stormed off to the room. Now I had to go in there and make things right with her. My pistol was on the floor, so I picked it up and went onto the room. Leilani was sitting on the bed eyeballing me hard, but she wasn't crying. I placed the gun on the dresser and walked over to the bed where she was sitting.

"Baby." I tried to grab her hands, but she moved them before I could touch her.

"I'm listening." Her stare was blank and she appeared to be apathetic about the situation.

"Crystal is a girl that I was dealing with when I met you, but the moment we started talking, I ended things with her and she wasn't happy about that. She came by here because she been texting me and I never respond."

"Yeah, 'cause I'm here, that's why you not responding." Leilani rolled her eyes so damn hard, I thought them muthafuckas was gone get stuck.

"That's a lie and you can bet that." I was getting a little frustrated because she didn't believe a nigga. "She just trying to ruin what I got going on 'cause she see a nigga happy without her."

"So, somebody you fucked a long time ago, just popped up to yo' place after all that time? That's bullshit."

"I'm tryin' to explain it to you."

"Did you fuck her?" she screamed and hit the bed with her hand.

I stepped closer to her, but she extended her arm between us to keep me away. "Baby, calm down please."

"Coy, answer my question or I'm leaving. Did you fuck her? Yes or no."

"Ugh." I rubbed my hands over my face. "Yeah."

"When?" She tilted her head to the side and looked me in my eyes. "Was it two months ago like she said? Yes or no."

"Yeah."

The room fell silent and all she did was stare at me for what seemed like forever. Leilani bit down on her lip and shook her head from side to side. I could see she was getting teary-eyed, but she held her head back like she was trying to hold them back.

"Leilani." She ignored me. "Baby, please say something." I gave her time to pull herself together.

Leilani finally looked at me. "So, you mean to tell me you fucked this girl around the same time you wined and dined and fucked me?"

"I didn't fuck you. I made love to you. There's a difference. I only fucked her 'cause I was drunk and not thinkin'."

By this time my voice elevated, but I was trying to keep my cool. I knew I was wrong, but damn, it only happened once. "That shit didn't mean nothing to me. I'm where I wanna be and I told her that while you was standing there. If I was still fuckin' her, do you think that shit would've played out like that?"

"I don't know what to think," she screamed. The tears she had been desperately holding back finally started to fall slowly down her cheeks.

"I gave you my most prized possession and you would do this to me? I trusted you. Everything you said earlier was a lie."

Damn! I really fucked up. Seeing her tear-stained face really fucked me up big time. I couldn't stand to see her crying and heartbroken behind something I did.

"Everything I said was the truth and you can still trust me," I pleaded.

"No. No. I can't." She shook her head from side to side.

The damage was done and all I could do was comfort her if she allowed it, so I tried my luck. I moved towards her slowly and gently took her into my arms. She didn't resist.

"Leilani, believe me when I say that it was a mistake and I never meant to hurt you." The more I apologized, the more emotional she became. Her shoulders started to bounce up and down and her sobbing grew louder by the second. I kissed the top of her head and inhaled the cocoa scent of her bone-straight, jet-black hair that stopped in the middle of her back.

"I can't take seeing you cry, please stop." I rubbed her back to calm her down, but that didn't work.

It took a long thirty minutes of begging, pleading and promising, to get her calm, but that was only half the battle. It was going to take a lot more to gain her trust once again.

"Let me go," she said, just above a whisper, while trying to squirm her way out of my grip.

"Why?"

"I need to get up for a minute."

I honored her request and gave her the space she needed to get up. Leilani eased from the bed, removed my boxers she was wearing and tossed them on the bed. The dress she had on earlier was on the floor. In silence, I watched her slip it over her slender frame. Her actions had me curious, but I didn't interrupt her, I just observed. She then slipped on her slides and began to gather her things.

"Leilani, what are you doing?" It was obvious, but I asked anyway.

"I need time away from you." She grabbed her overnight bag and tossed it over her shoulder. "Can you take me home please?" Her back was facing me.

"I can't do that. We need to work this out."

"I need time to think and I can't do that here." She turned her head halfway in my direction. "So again, can you take me home? If not, I'll find a way myself."

"No, I can't let you leave like this." When I grabbed her arm, she snatched it away from me.

"Stop! I'm leaving." Leilani stormed out the bedroom like she had fire under her ass, so I gave chase.

My strides were much larger than hers and allowed me to catch up to her quickly. If she thought she was leaving me, she had another muthafuckin' thang coming. I was on her heels. Leilani managed to unlock the door, but I caught her before she could open it. I snatched her by the arm aggressively and pulled her close to my body. "What the fuck did I just say? Yo' ass ain't going nowhere," I yelled in her face.

Chapter 5

Leilani

This nigga must've lost his rabbit ass mind, snatching me up like he crazy. I guess he didn't see what just happened to his ex bitch. If he didn't let me go in three point two-five seconds, I was gone go in his shit too.

"Let me go so I can go home. I'm not staying in here another minute with you." I was trying to break free, but his ass was cock-strong.

"No." he squeezed my arm tighter.

"Coy let me go and I'm not playing with you." My voice raised so he would know I was serious. "I'm telling you now. Let me go," I warned.

"You need to calm yo' hyper ass down." He tugged on my arm harder and tried pulling me to the room, but I wasn't about to give in to his demands. "Now, let's go back in the room so we can talk about this like adults. I'm not about to lose you behind something so stupid."

"I don't wanna talk to you." He tried to drag me and that was when I unleashed the beast on his ass.

I planted my feet hard against the floor, forcing down my weight and went wild, swinging on his ass. I caught him right in the mouth with a closed fist, drawing blood. He let me go.

"What the fuck wrong with you?" he shouted, so I shouted back.

"I told you to take me home and since you don't want to, I will find my own ride."

Coy licked his bottom lip, then ran his tongue across his teeth. He frowned. I guess he tasted the blood. His brow bent and his eyes darted in my direction. He slowly raised his hand to his mouth and touched it. There was blood on his fingertips. The stare in his eyes was cold and of pure evil and it made me feel a little uneasy. I was ready to flee and get far away from him as possible. Coy was swift and I couldn't duck fast enough before he slapped me in the face with a tremendous amount of force.

Whap!

My head snapped back, then forward like a bobble head doll. I immediately started to see stars as the pain settled in. I shook my head a few times trying to shake it off. Coy's eyes were red like the devil himself, as he stood there with his fists balled up. He was breathing so hard, his shoulders were moving up and down. My first thought was to run and that's exactly what I did. I snatched the front door open and tried to scurry out the apartment, but before I could get out the door, he grabbed a handful of my hair and snatched me back inside, slinging me to the floor.

Boom!

He slammed the door so hard, the walls shook. I would be lying if I said I wasn't scared. Like a mad man, he charged towards me and grabbed me by both of my arms.

"Stop!" I screamed, but my sounds fell on deaf ears.

Coy started dragging me across the carpet, while I kicked and screamed.

"Stooopppp! Let me go."

"Shut the fuck up!" he yelled, while dragging me down the hall by my arms.

The friction between my skin and the carpet was hot, but I continued to kick and rock my body so he could let me go. I didn't know this person. It was like he just flipped out on me in the blink of an eye.

"My legs are burning," I cried.

"Fuck yo' legs. Now you'll think twice about trying to leave me." He dragged me to the middle of the bedroom floor and let me go. "I'll break them shits and immobilize yo' ass. Now try me."

I heard his threat loud and clear, but the fact remained the same, I wanted out. My father didn't raise me to take beatings from a man. I got up from the floor and faced him.

"Just let me leave. You took it too far."

"And you didn't?"

"You know," I sighed. "At this point, it doesn't matter. I'm done. This relationship is over."

Coy closed his eyes and took a deep breath. When he opened them, he stepped closer, invading my personal space. "You wanna leave me?"

Just the utterance of the word *yes* set him off. Coy snapped and started slapping me across the face. That sent me into straight attack mode. I was swinging, punching, clawing and biting him. He was able to slam me onto the bed and restrain me by straddling my waist.

"Stop," he shouted, damn near out of breath.

I couldn't hold back my tears any longer, as I looked into the eyes of the man who was supposed to love me and not hurt me. "Let me go. I don't wanna be with you anymore," I screamed loudly.

My arms were pinned down to the bed and the only thing I could move were my legs. My teardrops slid down into my ears. The sight of him made me nauseous. His eyes went from hard to soft, as they glistened.

"Leilani, be still please. I don't want to hurt you."

"Too late for that." I continued to squirm underneath his frame, so he laid on top of me. "It's over," I repeated.

Coy used his knee to push one of my legs open. I struggled to keep him from going further, but he was too heavy and strong for me. He was able to push them open and mount himself in between them.

"Coy, stop please," I begged. He freed one of my arms and I could feel his hand on my thigh. "If you love me, you would stop."

Coy rubbed his semi-stiff dick against my lips before shoving all eleven inches inside of me. "Stooppp," I cried.

With my free hand, I tried to push him off of me, but he grabbed it and pinned it back to the bed. All I could do was just lay there and cry, while he thrusted in and out of my dry-ass vagina. The friction alone was killing me.

"I'm sorry, Leilani, but I can't let you go and I'll kill anybody that tries to get in the way of that." He kissed the side of my face. "You just don't understand the amount of damage I could cause if you leave me."

I felt violated, being forced to have sex against my will, but I knew this was his way of manipulating me and altering my mental state. He grinded on me slowly like it made a difference. This was not lovemaking.

"I love you, Leilani, and I'm sorry for hitting you." He tried to kiss me in the mouth, but I turned my head. "I just wanna make you feel good." He kissed my cheek. "Ooh, she so wet."

In my mind, I was turned off, but my body was addicted to his touch and singing another tune. I didn't care how wet it was or how easily he was able to glide in and out with ease I wasn't enjoying it. I just laid there motionless without a sound. To take my mind off of the physical and now sexual abuse I went back to my happier days.

"Good job, princess," my father shouted in excitement. "All the numbers are accurate." He kissed me on the cheek. "My baby a genius."

Every weekend, I accompanied him to his job and that's when he taught me how to keep up with his books at nine years old.

"Thank you." I smiled. "I learned from the best." He made sure I attended prestigious schools to make sure I was highly educated.

"That's right. It's important to be able to count big numbers. That way, no one could cheat you out your money. Accountants are nothing but scam artists and they can't be trusted. They'll rob you blind for years and by the time you figure it out, they'll be repossessing your cars and foreclosing on your home."

He picked up his briefcase and keys from the desk. "Let's get out of here. Oh, before I forget, here." He pulled out a crispy, one-hundred-dollar-bill and handed it to me.

"Thank you, Daddy." I was cheesing hard.

"Always get paid for the work you do. Nothing in this world is free. Got it?"

"Yes." I nodded my head.

"Now, let's go and deposit that into your account and grab some lunch."

The vivid image of me and my father suddenly disappeared when I felt Coy get off me. I was relieved and finally able to breathe without restraints. He laid down beside me and put his arm across my stomach. "Let's dream together."

Coy pulled me close to his chest and put one leg over me. He wanted to make sure I didn't get up while he slept. After lying there for a while, I eventually dozed off with him.

***

"So, wait a minute. You mean to tell me sweet, respectable Coy cheated on you?" Caussia gaped as I ran down the details of the fight with his ex-girlfriend, Crystal.

I intentionally left out the fight between us, because we were still together. He had my heart and I couldn't walk away so easily. We sat down and discussed what went down and I forgave him. I can admit things did get out of hand and I started the fight. So, moving forward, we agreed to keep our hands to ourselves.

"Yes."

"The sweet Coy who won your daddy over, cheated on you?" Caussia was in disbelief.

"That would be him," I replied.

"The one you lost your virginity to?"

"Yes, girl, for the last time." I laughed it off. I wasn't over it and it still hurt, but eventually, I would have to build a bridge and get over it. "You just gone run it into the ground, huh?"

"I just can't believe it, that's all." Caussia scooped some ice cream from her bowl and stuffed her face.

"Girl, me either. I was mad at him and not her, but when she called me a bitch the second time and said she wasn't leaving, I had to molly wop that ho' and teach her about trying me."

Caussia's laugh was loud and straight from the belly. "Girl, I wish I was there to witness that. I know she wished she would've did a background check before coming over there with that bullshit."

"Well, she know now." I laughed. "It's going to be hard to trust him again."

My head dropped and I became so focused on Caussia's socks on the floor. I was in my feelings once again. "How am I supposed to trust him from another state, if I can't do it in the same county?"

Coy didn't realize how much he hurt me with that one. It felt like he took my heart out my chest and stepped on it with a pair of Timberland boots.

"Giiiirl, we about to be in another state with a boatload of ball players. I wouldn't sweat that for one second. I'll give you until the second semester and I bet you'll forget all about him."

I cut my eyes at her. "I lost my virginity to him. It's not like there isn't a connection. This happened on my birthday and he made that day special for me."

"There's no statute that says we will be with our firsts forever. Sometimes, we just have to suck it up and move on."

I laid back onto the bed and looked up at the ceiling. That immediately gave me a flashback about the mirror on the ceiling. "That's easy for you to say, 'cause you lost your virginity to someone you wasn't dating and in his parents' truck at that."

Caussia sat her bowl down on the floor. "Hey, hey don't try to downplay my first time." She giggled and laid next to me. "That was my choice and it was good too."

My mouth started to water and the room seemed like it was spinning. I jumped up quickly and rushed into the bathroom. I lifted the toilet seat and threw up the Chinese food I had eaten earlier. Caussia walked in and stood next to me.

"Are you okay?" I held my arm up 'cause I couldn't respond. It felt like I was throwing my guts up. "Ooh, you pregnant, ain't it?"

I shook my head no and continued to empty out the contents in my stomach. When I was done, I leaned away from the toilet and took a few short, quick breaths.

"Leilani, you pregnant?"

"No. We use condoms, so that ain't possible. It had to be that nasty ass food I ate. It was probably a rat or some shit."

"Come on, silly, because I've been eating there for years." Caussia helped me up from the floor. "Your toothbrush in the cabinet."

After I cleaned myself up, I went back into the room and laid down. "What are you wearing to your party?"

"This Gucci outfit Coy got for me." The night of the fight he gave me fifteen hundred dollars to go shopping. I saw that as a way to pay for cheating and to keep me quiet about it.

"Where do he get that type of money from to just be throwing it around like that?" She stared at me in bewilderment.

"You know he works for his uncle."

Caussia smirked. "Now, you know damn well his crooked-ass uncle don't own a single business."

"He has that recording studio."

She cracked up. "Who the hell he producing, 'cause I ain't seen a single artist blow up or even drop a mixtape. This nigga riding around in a Hummer with that fake-ass logo on it."

"Girl, you stupid."

"I know."

Between all of the gossiping and laughter, we both fell asleep. A few hours later, I was awakened by a tap on my shoulder.

"Leilani, your ride is here."

I stirred from my sleep, blinking a few times to see who just interrupted my nap. It was Caussia's mom.

"Your boyfriend is here to pick you up."

"Okay." I yawned, while sitting up.

My nap was good, but I was ready to go back to Coy's place and sleep. But, I knew that wasn't happening with his overly horny ass. I got up and went outside to find him sitting in the car, talking on the phone. He hung up when I opened the door.

"Why you hung up so suddenly?" I closed the door and put on my seatbelt.

"My conversation was over. What you talm 'bout?"

"Nothing, let's go. I'm sleepy."

Coy leaned close to me. "I missed you. Give me a kiss." I gave him a sorry, weak-ass peck. "Nah, I didn't like that. I need some tongue action."

Of course, I gave in with no hesitation. He placed his hand between my legs and massaged my kitty through my jeans, making her moist. Coy pulled back and broke our kiss.

"My shit hard." He looked down and smiled. "See, that's what you do to me. I'm horny as fuck."

"When are you not horny?"

Coy laughed. "Shit, I'm always horny, ain't no shame in that." He backed out the driveway slowly. "You want food before we go in?"

"Yeah."

"What you want?"

"Surprise me."

"I'll surprise you wit' some dick on a platter, so you better answer." When he started to hum it made me laugh. He could be so goofy at times. "Ooh girl, I gotta get you home with me tonight." His singing was horrible.

"Yeah, I bet you can't, nasty ass. I'm sleepy."

He looked at me with those puppy eyes. "Can I get some head tonight please? You never do me and I eat yo' shit faithfully."

I sunk low in my seat. That was something I didn't care to engage in. "That's nasty."

"You nasty, 'cause you wanna be the only one gettin' oral pleasure and that's not fair. As a woman, you supposed to please your man, so he don't go outside of his home." He dropped his head and gave me a sad puppy dog look. "Pleease," he begged.

My mind went back to when he cheated and it made me wonder if it *was my fault* he slept with his ex. I mean, I guess it wouldn't hurt to try it, but I don't see how all of that would fit in my mouth. I gagged just at the thought. Hell, I don't even like bananas, so I didn't see how that was going to work. However, I was willing to try it if that would make him happy. I kept quiet for a little while longer, before I answered him.

"I guess I can try it if that will make you happy."

Coy started smiling hard and I could see all of the teeth in his head. Then, he started rocking from side to side. "Ooh, the boy done came up. I'm finally getting' some head after begging for years."

"Hush, silly. We haven't been together a year yet."

I swear, he didn't waste any time picking up food and getting us back his apartment. He damn near ran every light and all he kept saying was, "let me hurry up before you change your mind." I swear, the man was crazy, but I loved him though.

Chapter 6

Leilani

Tonight, I was celebrating the beginning of a new chapter in my life. I was officially out of high school and preparing myself to leave home and venture out into the real world on my own. I remember dreaming about moving out and getting my own place. Finally, that dream had become a reality and I was overjoyed. My father threw me a graduation party and a going-away party at the same time at the Firefighter Hall, since I was scheduled to leave in a week for college.

My party was going down in history and all of my friends were in the building, showing their girl some love. Me and my best friend, Caussia, were hyped, singing along to Missy Elliot's "All in my Grill," bouncing in front of each other.

"This party dope as fuck, Leilani," Caussia screamed over the music.

"I know, right? A bitch can't tell me shit. Fuck they thought." I smiled, twirling my hips.

Talk is talk, and talk is cheap
Tell it to her, don't say it to me
'cause I know I'm in control
See Trix are for kids, and boo, I'm too old
Go 'head, with your games
Don't ever come back to me again
Where you go, remember me
I'm the best thing in history.

On that last note, I flipped my hair and smirked in the direction of Coy. I was feeling that shit in my soul. I was still hurt because he had the audacity to cheat with some bum-ass bitch he used to fuck before I came into the picture. This nigga needed to know I was a boss-ass bitch and all these other hoes were beneath me, except my girl, Caussia. His ass needed to recognize it was an honor to have me on his shoulder in the first place.

Coy was heated. I could tell by the way his top lip curled and that pit-bull mug he used to intimidate people was plastered on his face. He wasn't slow, so he knew I was singing this for his ass. I didn't care, because it was my night and I was fly as fuck in my Gucci 'fit that he paid for. I promised him I would work on forgiveness, but this ho' had the nerve to text him earlier and now I felt like he made up with her. *Why else would she text him after he let me beat her ass?*

"Boy, bye!" I mouthed, then waved my hand like I was sending him on his way. As soon as I did that, he pulled himself from the wall and stormed towards me in swift, long strides until he was in my face.

Caussia stepped to the side after he bumped into her and looked him up and down with her lips tooted up. "Excuse you rude ass. What you bum rushing a bitch for?"

Coy didn't bother to look in her direction, because he was too busy staring in my face, breathing like a goddamn dragon. "Shut up and go find a dick to suck, you ho'."

"Fuck you, wit'cho ho' ass. Out here giving up that community dick," she clapped back with no problem.

"Ho', shut the fuck up, befo' I make you suck this community dick in front of yo' best friend."

That shit made me snap on his ass, 'cause my bestie was the furthest thing from a ho. "Don't talk to my friend like that. What the fuck is your problem?" I rolled my eyes and neck. "I swear, you so fuckin' disrespectful and you don't care, but let that would've been me saying some shit like that to one of your homeboys, it would be a problem."

Coy grabbed me tightly by the arm and squeezed it, pulling me close to him. The glare in his eyes was scary, as he spoke through clenched teeth. "Yo', who the fuck you think you talkin' to like that? You better check that mouth of yours and ya' homegirl shit, before I do it for you."

Caussia's mouth fell open in surprise. She had never seen him act this way before and I never told her he hit me before. So, instead of making a scene and getting my father involved I turned down the hostility in my voice to calm the inner beast. "Coy let's talk about this outside." I pleaded.

"Nah, let's do this shit right here, since you got all that muthafuckin' mouth and you smelling that young, hot-ass pussy between yo' legs." He wasn't loud, but there was enough volume in his voice for a few heads to turn.

Placing my free hand on his shoulder, I whispered softly. "People are starting to stare, so stop making a scene before my daddy come over here and we both know that won't end well."

I tried my best to hide my fear and ignore the cold, hard stare from his eyes, but I didn't know what to expect. Not once did he blink. He stood there in deep thought for a few seconds, before he loosened his grip. "You better stop trying me and I'm dead-ass serious." The harshness in his words was no surprise.

"What are you talking about? All I'm doing is dancing and singing, so stop acting stupid," I replied.

"You know what I'm talking about. You always trying to use a song to express the way you feel 'bout shit, instead of opening yo' mouth."

Just as I was about to answer him, the music stopped and all I could hear was the chatter from everyone talking. A loud beeping sound from the microphone pierced our ears, taking our attention to the stage. When I looked up, I saw my dad standing up there, so I made my way towards the front so he could see me.

"Can I get everybody's attention, please?" His baritone voice echoed through the speakers silencing the crowd. "As we all know, today is a special day for my princess and the happiest day of my life," he chuckled. "Well, next to the day she came into this world."

The love I had for my daddy was unexplainable, since our bond was tighter than a fat bitch in spandex. It felt good to make him proud and accomplish everything we planned. I often thought back to that night I came clean to him about my mother.

If I would've kept my mouth closed, only God knows where I would be right now. The very next day, my father received a call that the client he was supposed to meet up with was killed, along with his family, with the exception of one son that got away, in a home invasion. I still cried to this very day, because my courage saved his life.

The relationship between me and my surrogate was never repaired. She had to do one year in rehab before she was allowed to come back home. The day she stepped foot in the house, he laid down the ground rules about respecting each other and that was as far as our relationship went. The scars she left on my heart with her words were far worse than the physical abuse and I couldn't find the strength to forgive her. They never got a divorce, so I had to live with that.

"Leilani, you have made your father the happiest man alive and there is nothing in this world I won't do for you. To see you work hard and maintain a 4.5 GPA says a lot about me as a father. I swear, I cried when you gave your valedictorian speech."

The crowd drowned him out with their oohs and aww's.

"It pleases me to see you walking in my footsteps and attending Harvard University, to pursue your dream as a criminal defense attorney. I'm proud of you, baby, and I have a surprise for you."

My daddy sat the microphone down and walked off the stage. I was standing by the steps when he approached me and gave me a hug.

"I love you, Daddy," I whispered, with my head buried into his chest.

"I love you too, sweetheart." After he let me go, he handed me a small box. "The world is yours baby."

Opening up the box, I just knew I was getting more diamonds, but to my surprise, it was a set of keys. Instantly, I jumped up and down in excitement. "Daddy, where is it?" I screeched.

"Outside, let's go and see."

When I glanced to the left, my surrogate was leaned against the wall, all standoffish with a smug look on her face. I swear, nothing I did made that woman happy. I could become the first female president and she wouldn't acknowledge my success. It used to bother me, because I couldn't understand why my bond with my father was an issue. I even went as far as researching her behavior to gain a better understanding. It was disturbing to learn that she viewed me as the other woman. *What the fuck do me and my father look like sleeping with each other?* Nor was it my fault she didn't go to college and better herself, instead of being a stay-at-home mother. That was her decision, not mine. I swear that bitch needed a head check, 'cause she acted like I was her step-daughter or some shit. Sometimes it made me wonder if she loved me at all.

As we walked off, my surrogate followed behind us without a single word, with her mean ass. I was certain she was still upset with Aniya for getting married at seventeen and moving to New York with her husband to pursue her dreams as a dance instructor.

I found it quite entertaining, since she was the one encouraging Aniya to go against my father's wishes and make her own decisions. In the middle of the night, she told me goodbye. I watched Aniya get into her boyfriend's car and never look back. The next morning, Diane found the letter she left behind and passed out. They kept her in the hospital for three days.

Butterflies were rumbling on the inside of my stomach like crazy, as he opened up the door for me to walk out. After taking a few steps towards the curb, that's when I noticed this sexy-ass, white BMW with a huge red bow on it. I completely lost my composure, jumping up and down, while giving my father another hug.

"Thank you, Daddy. I love it," I cried out with joy and excitement.

"You're welcome, baby."

Amongst the crowd, I could see Caussia standing next to Coy with a huge smile on her face. I guess the both of them had calmed down by now. One thing I could say about her, she was always genuine when it came down to our friendship, and vice versa.

I waved my hand in their direction and shouted, "Y'all come on so I can test drive it." They both walked towards the car and Coy opened the door, so Caussia could climb into the back of my two-seater.

"Come right back," my father shouted. Then he turned towards the crowd and sent them back on the inside.

I was so happy cranking up my dream car and pulling out into the road. "This a bad-ass ride, best friend. Now we twinning." She laughed.

"I know, right? Make me think they got a special on both of these cars." I came to a stop sign, looked both ways then pulled off. Caussia's daddy was a district attorney and both of our families were really close. We often ate dinner together and listened to them talk about the justice system and the criminal cases they handled. Just a few weeks ago, her daddy presented her with the same car, but it was black.

Coy hadn't said a word since he got inside the car, so I knew he was still pissed off. "Are you going to say anything? Or you gone just sit there and have an attitude for the rest of the night?"

He was silent for a minute. Then, he finally parted his lips to respond. "So, when you gone tell yo' daddy you not going off to college?"

"Um. Um," I stuttered. "I was waiting on the right time. He's been so happy lately and I didn't want to ruin that."

Caussia poked her head from the back seat. "What you mean, you not going to college? Our whole lives have been set up for us and you changing your mind about that?"

"I want to stay here and go to school. Coy and I are moving in together." I knew she was going to be disappointed to hear me say that, but not more than my daddy, once he heard the news.

"Caussia, why can't you just mind your business sometimes, damn!" Coy was annoyed with her and he didn't mind letting her know it. "You always have something to say."

"She's my best friend and it's my job to let her know when she fuckin' up, since yo' selfish ass ain't gone say it." I could see her rolling her eyes in the rear view mirror.

"Leilani, if the relationship is meant to be then it will work itself out, but don't ruin your future for him. It ain't like he faithful to you anyway and he not about to marry you. He only gave you that promise ring to make you think it's going to happen."

Caussia was right about the cheating part, but there was something else she didn't know and I could've slapped his ass for bringing this up right now. This was supposed to be a special night for me and he was doing his best to sabotage it.

"This the shit I'm talkin' 'bout, right there. Why do you constantly tell her our business?"

"She is my best friend." He knew that from day-one, so I don't know why he acting all crazy out the blue like that.

This nigga completely spazzed out. "I get it. I fuckin' get it, but damn, how many times you gon' keep saying that best friend shit? That's irritating as fuck."

"Maybe you should find you one, 'cause clearly you need somebody to converse with." Caussia stuck her tongue out and laughed. I swear, she could be so childish at times.

"Caussia, stop, 'cause you making it worse." The both of them knew how to drive me crazy, but I loved them. I just couldn't make them get along.

"Fuck him. Now again, why you not going to Harvard? The most prestigious school in the country, 'cause I'm a tad bit confused and disturbed by it all."

"Disrespect me one more time and watch I slap fire from yo' ass."

"You ain't gone do shit to me."

Coy turned towards the back seat like he was about to hit her, so I slammed down hard on the brakes. Both of their bodies jerked forward. No one was wearing a seatbelt.

"Just stop, damn. Y'all are making me crazier than what I already am," I screamed to the top of my lungs, trying to get my point across. I hit the steering wheel with my fist and started crying. I mean, I was bawling like a child.

At any moment, I knew I was going to have a meltdown. All of this was happening too fast and this was not how I planned on breaking the news. For the first time, they remained silent. I had to get away from them, so I got out the car to get some fresh air. I stood behind the car, placed both hands on the trunk and released a horrific scream. Seconds later, I heard the car door close.

Caussia stood beside me and rubbed the middle of my back. "I'm sorry, Leilani. I didn't mean to upset you like this." I was so pissed off, I couldn't respond. "I don't know what's going on with you, but you are making a huge mistake. This has been our lifelong dream since we were kids and I hate to see you ruin it, just because you think he's the one for you."

There was no doubt she didn't have my best interest at heart, but what I needed right now was space, so I could get my mind right. We never kept secrets from one another, but Coy thought it was best we kept our business private. He constantly reminded me that I didn't have to tell her everything and some things should stay between us.

"You just don't understand what I'm going through. This is really hard for me and I don't need judgement from anyone. Not you, Coy, or my father."

On the inside, I was broken, torn and confused on the decision I wanted to make. No matter what I chose, in the end, someone was going to be hurt.

"I've never judged you," Caussia stated in her defense. "All I'm saying is *think* about your future. If you and Coy break up, then what? You can't get that time back."

Sudden movement caught my attention and when I opened up my eyes, I could see Coy's feet next to me. So, I stood up. "What you back here telling her? And who said we breaking up?"

"I didn't tell her anything," I snapped. "And, I wish both of y'all would shut the fuck up, 'cause this bickering and fighting is getting on my nerves."

Coy grabbed me by both arms and shook me like a rag doll. "I told you to watch yo' fuckin' mouth and you steady tryin' me. Don't show out in front of this bitch and get fucked up."

"Coy, let her go," Caussia shouted.

To my surprise, he did. I was a tad bit dizzy, so I reached out to grab ahold of the car to keep from falling. Instantly, I felt sick and everything I had eaten at the party was on its way back up. I leaned to the side to release the contents left behind in my stomach. Coy jumped back in the nick of time and I missed getting vomit on his shoes by a few inches. But, he quickly stepped in and held my hair out of my face. It felt like I had just threw my guts up.

"Leilani, are you okay?" Caussia panicked.

"No." I was still crying, so he held me up. "I'm pregnant."

"Leilani!" Caussia cried out with me. "I knew it, but how could you let this happen? We talked about this."

My voice cracked while I answered her. "It just happened. I mean, what else am I supposed to do?"

"Get an abortion, 'cause if you don't, your daddy is gonna be pissed with you." She made a valid point, but I was a daddy's girl and he loved me unconditionally.

"What the fuck you mean, get an abortion?" Coy barked, snapping his head to the side. "She ain't killing my muthafuckin' baby, so stop trying to put that bullshit in her head." He was heated, so he walked me to the passenger side. "Let's go."

"You are one selfish son of a bitch." She mean-mugged Coy hard as fuck. "And I can't believe you letting this nigga ruin your fuckin' life."

I didn't respond to her, because it hurt to know I didn't have the support from the one person I knew had my back on everything. Coy got in the driver's seat and drove us back. I used that time to pull myself together.

As we pulled back up to the venue, my father and my surrogate were standing outside, waiting on us to return.

Coy looked over at me with this mean look on his face. "You better tell them now, before I do it for you."

"Coy, we can do this tomorrow," I whined like a baby, not wanting to ruin such a perfect night.

"Do it now, or you can forget about us forever and I promise you, I won't do shit for that baby," he threatened.

"Coy, please." I placed my hand gently on his arm so I could reason with him. "Let's just do this tomorrow in private at the house. We don't need everybody in our business. I'm sick and I don't have the energy to deal with this tonight. I just want to go home and sleep. I made my final decision and tomorrow we can tell him together. I love you, okay?"

The hardened look on his face softened and his breathing slowed down when he looked deep into my soul—damn—my eyes. "Okay," he whispered, then wiped the fresh tears from my face. "I love you too and I'm sorry for blowing up back there." To seal the deal, he pop kissed me on the mouth, despite the fact that I was throwing up not too long ago.

"It's okay, baby. We're all just frustrated." We were finally able to get out the car and proceed with our night. Caussia didn't say a single word to me. Instead, she walked past us and went back on the inside.

My daddy was smiling when I walked up to him, but it suddenly disappeared when he saw my face. "What's the matter, sweetheart?"

My heart was racing like he could see through me and knew all about my secret. "I don't feel good and I'm ready to go."

"Okay, that's fine. Just go inside and tell your guests goodnight."

My father put his arm around my shoulder and escorted me back inside the building. I was sick as a dog, literally and emotionally. He had already warned me and Coy about bringing a baby home and we were doing just that. Tomorrow, I was going to break his heart, but I was hoping and praying he wouldn't be too harsh when he got the news. After all, I was his baby, his twin, his protégé and number-one girl, all wrapped up into one.

Chapter 7

Leilani

As we sat in my car, my hands trembled and I was scared to death about what was about to happen. I have never disappointed my father in life, but today was going to be that day. I was trying to get my nerves in check, but nothing I did before I got there worked.

"Come on and let's get this over with." Coy opened the car door. "You act like he gon' kill us."

"That's easy for you to say. You are not in my shoes."

"Damn near. Shit, he told both of us the same thing and I'm sure he's going to blame me for you getting pregnant in the first place." Coy grabbed my hand. "Listen, we are doing this together, so stop worrying. He can only be so mad for so long. That man loves you too much to just cut you off completely."

"That's what you think. He hasn't spoken to my sister since she left."

"Y'all are two different people. You and him got a unbreakable bond, so I just don't see that happening. You his favorite child."

I got out the car and closed the door. My legs felt like they just wanted to run away from this house and disappear for good. I unlocked the door and walked inside. My father and surrogate were cuddled up on the couch watching television. We walked in and I sat down on the same exact sofa we were grilled on previously. Coy approached my daddy.

He moved his arm from around Diane and they both sat up. "What's up, you two?"

"Not much. We just left from having lunch on the Intercoastal."

"Must be nice." He laughed.

Coy shook hands with my dad and surrogate before he came and sat down beside me.

"How you feeling today, baby?"

"I'm feeling much better."

"That's good." My father leaned forward, resting his arms on his thighs. I could tell he was trying to read our body language. "Why y'all look so tense and serious?" He paused and looked deeper. "Don't tell me y'all done snuck off and got hitched."

Coy laughed. "Nah, not yet. But, we do need to talk to you about something important."

"Okay, shoot it." We had his undivided attention, along with the surrogate.

Coy grabbed my hand, interlocking our fingers. "Go ahead, baby, tell him."

I sat there in silence, trying to find the courage to confess, but being in his presence made that damn near impossible to do. He meant everything to me and at that moment, I wanted to tell Coy I wanted to have the abortion instead. We could always have a baby later on in life.

My mouth opened, but the words didn't come out at all. I was mute. I didn't know how to articulate my words and say what needed to be said, so I just sat there, playing with the keys in my hand.

"Talk to me, Leilani, what's going on?" he asked.

My inner voice starting talking again. *Get ready to kill your father, stupid. Everything he taught and did for your dumb ass was all in vain!*

Taking a deep breath, I swallowed my fears and prepared myself to deliver the most devastating news in my entire life. "Daddy, I'm pregnant."

My eyes went straight to my feet to keep from making eye contact. I was ashamed and I couldn't look him in the eyes, knowing that I disappointed him. "I'm sorry, Daddy."

Tears fell from my eyes and hit the tile. To me, it sounded like a huge splash. No one said a word, but I could sense the tension in the air without looking. And, it was taking longer than I expected to receive some type of response, so I looked up to see what he was doing. We made eye contact and I could feel his eyes burning a hole through my sinful soul.

"What the fuck you mean, you pregnant?" That response let me know the old "Leonard from the block" was in the building. The new one didn't talk that way. As expected, Diane just sat there in silence. She seemed so nonchalant. "I just had this conversation with y'all a few weeks ago. I specifically said, don't bring any babies to this house."

His eyes darted in Coy's direction. "I told you to make sure you used condoms with my daughter, since I couldn't stop y'all from fuckin'."

"Mr. J, I kept my word and did that," Coy replied.

"Not if she pregnant, you didn't."

"Daddy," I needed to continue to put emphasis on that word to try and keep him calm. "It's true. We have been using condoms. When I went to the doctor, she confirmed I was two months. This happened the night I lost my virginity." I tried to shed light on the situation, so he didn't think Coy didn't honor his wish.

"I don't care when it happened, and you not having no muthafuckin' baby, so I advise the both of you to locate the nearest abortion clinic and get rid of the mess you created."

Coy spoke up without hesitation. "With all due respect, Mr. J, but we keeping the baby."

He pointed his finger in Coy's direction. "Who the fuck are you to determine what my daughter is going to do?"

"Leilani is grown now and she can make her own decisions, and this is one that we made together."

My father looked at Diane. "Did you know about this?" His bark was big, but his bite was much bigger.

Diane shook her head from side to side. "I didn't know anything and you know she don't talk to me. That's your child and you would've seen it coming, had you not put her up on a pedestal so damn high, you could've seen what she was doing. You act as if she's your only child. We do have another daughter out here."

"Aniya made her bed and now she gets to lay in it every night the way she sees fit."

"And apparently, so did Leilani." She sat back and folded her arms across her chest.

My father turned his attention back to me. "So, all of a sudden you wanna be a teenage mother, with no education, food stamps and living on housing?"

"No." I shook my head. "After I have the baby, I will finish school."

"Do you hear how stupid that sounds? Do you know how many young girls say that same dumb-ass shit and never go back until they're thirty? Raising a baby is hard and what you gone do when he leaves you to be a single parent? Have you thought that far into it, because I don't think you did?"

"Mr. J, I know you're upset—"

My father cut him off. "Oh, you have no idea."

"You should know I love Leilani dearly and I want us to get married. There's no way I would leave her to be a single mother. You said a man's job is to take care of his family, be their provider and protector, and that's exactly what I'm doing. Leilani will have the baby and after that, she will go to school."

My father jumped to his feet. "You don't run shit over here. I do. I'm the king in this muthafuckin' castle and she gone get rid of that baby."

"I agree that you are the king in your castle and I respect that, but I'm the king in mine and I run that. So, she will be keeping my baby." Coy was too cocky for his own good and I was pulling his arm trying to make him be quiet, but he ignored me.

All I could see next was my daddy run up on him and take a swing. Coy tried to avoid being hit by moving, but he was caught in the jaw. His body flew backwards into the couch.

My daddy glared down at him with a hard piercing stare. "When I met yo' ass, I told you I had high expectations for my daughter."

He then turned to me. "And you, I thought you were smarter than this. How you let this nigga trap you like this? I got something for that ass." He walked towards the credenza.

Coy was holding his jaw when he sat up. "That's how you gon' disrespect me? By puttin' yo' hands on me?" He stood up like he was about to do something. "Nigga, I ain't never disrespect you like that."

"Coy, stop." I grabbed his arm, but he snatched away from me.

"Get the fuck off me." He slapped my hand away and took a few steps away from the couch. His breathing was rapid and his chest was heaving up and down.

My father turned back to face us clutching a Glock 40 and he aimed it at Coy. A piercing scream escaped my lips, as I held my hand over my mouth.

"Daddy, please don't hurt him. I love him and I'm going to be with him," I begged, silently praying that he wouldn't kill him.

"I'm not gone hurt him. I'm a kill his ass." Coy froze in place when he realized shit had just gotten real. "Run up if you want to, l'il nigga. I'll pump ya' ass wit' some hot lead babies. Don't let that suit and tie shit fool you, nigga. I'm a thoroughbred, born and raised in the muthafuckin' hood. Dope money sent me to law school."

I was stuck in place and it felt as if I was being held down, but I had to stop my daddy from shooting the father of my child. Soon enough, I was able to move, standing in between the gun and Coy.

"Move, Leilani," my father instructed.

With a painful cry suffocating my words, I managed to find my voice to get my point across.

"Daddy, please, just stop! Killing him isn't going to solve anything. It's not his fault and he didn't force me to do anything. This was my decision, so please just let me live my life and after I have the baby, I promise I will go to school."

To my surprise, Diane stood up and walked towards my dad, placing her hand over my father's hand, slowly pushing it down until his hand was at his side.

"Leonard, baby, put the gun away because to me, it sounds like she has given this a lot of thought and there's nothing you can do to stop her. And, I'm not losing you behind something so stupid. She's eighteen now and it's time to let her go, so she could learn from her mistakes. When he's done using her and bringing home other illegitimate children, she'll come running back with her tail between her legs, begging us to let her in."

My daddy looked me in my eyes and that was the moment I knew he was disappointed in me without a doubt. I hurt him deeply. The evidence was present in his penetrating stare. He slowly lowered his gun.

"Leilani, your mother is right. It's your decision, but I'm telling you now, if you don't go to college next week and you decide to keep that bastard of a child, you are on your own." He shook his head. "I promise you that."

"I'm sorry, Daddy." I walked up to him and hugged him tightly for what I felt was temporary and he didn't reciprocate. "Please don't hate me. I love you."

As I turned to walk away, I grabbed Coy by the hand and pulled him in the opposite direction of where my father was standing.

"Leave this house and you will never be able to step foot in here again."

We stopped and I turned to look him. Tears were pouring down my face. I knew he was upset with me, but I knew we would get past this. It was going to take some time, but I was optimistic. By the time I gave birth, we would be happy again. I just wished he could be a little more understanding.

"Daddy, please let me live my life." It hurt me to walk away, but I loved Coy and I wanted to have his baby.

"No problem. Give me the house keys and the keys to your car and tomorrow morning, you will be removed from all accounts and your credit cards will be canceled. I hope he can provide for you the way I did."

"Let her keep the car. I'm sure she's going to need it," Diane added, to my surprise.

"You right about that. So, moving forward, I will not be paying your car note or insurance. I'm sure your man can handle paying eight hundred and eighty-seven dollars a month for you to drive his baby around town. And, to make sure he does, I will be removing my name tomorrow and placing it solely in your name. I'm not getting a repo behind this."

I removed the house key and placed it on the arm of the chair, then I walked away. The last thing I heard was Diane's voice.

"I always told you she would be the one to hurt you and break your heart, but I didn't know what I was talking about. She chose dick over you."

Not knowing what the future was going to bring, I put my faith in Coy, praying he would be the man that I needed him to be.

We were a few feet from the front door, so I stopped. "Wait for me outside. I have a few things I need to get from upstairs."

"Okay." Coy walked out the front door as I was headed to my bedroom.

"What you need from upstairs?" I paused when I heard my father's voice.

"My clothes," I said softly.

"I'm sorry, baby, but anything my money paid for is not leaving my residence."

He was so angry and I hated the way he was looking at me. "Daddy, please don't do this to me. I'm still your princess, I've just gotten older and life has changed my situation, but I promise I won't let this hinder my education and growth. Just give me a chance to show you."

Deep down inside, I knew he didn't want to let me go. The water in his eyes told me so, but he was trying his best to fight it.

"Leilani, baby, I love you and I've shown you that for eighteen years, but I have to let you go. As a father, I've done all I could do to provide you the proper tools and advantages that you will need in life to become an educated black woman. I've invested thousands of dollars into your education from the time you could say *Daddy* at a young age, and now your irresponsible ways are about to cost me a hundred and seventy thousand for your tuition."

Hearing him say he had to let me go shattered my heart. I just wanted him to stand by me when I needed him the most. "Daddy, please, don't let me go," I cried. "I need you."

"If you needed me, you wouldn't be on your way out that door for good. Seems to me you need him more than the man that raised you and gave you the world. If I would've predicted this, I would've never let you date him in the first place. But no, I was trying to keep you from sneaking out by giving you just a little bit of freedom. I don't know where I went wrong with you."

"You didn't go wrong. It's still me," I pleaded. "I just made a mistake."

"Mistakes are easy to fix." He pointed at my stomach. "I'm not mad about that mistake, because that would only cost me about three hundred dollars. Not going to college is not a mistake. It's a foolish choice. Maybe I should've just made you wear a chastity belt."

"Daddy, this is my baby we're talking about, and he or she is not a mistake. You taught me babies were a blessing and no man had the right to tell a woman to end that life. What you're doing right now is the same thing Grandpa did to you. He didn't want his daughter to have any babies either, but you proved to him you were a man of your word. Let Coy prove he could be a provider like you."

"He couldn't be me if I sold him the manual and took his ass to class. I was born this way." He nodded his head. "I have to give that young nigga credit though. After all that training, drilling and teaching you the game of life for eighteen years, he was able to come in and deactivate your whole thought process in seven months. If it was the sex, then two months. He must have diamonds and gold between his legs or some shit, because he fucked you senseless."

My father never spoke to me in that manner. His words left me confused and feeling unloved. I just stood there and cried, hoping he would have a change of heart, but I was wrong.

"Stop crying." He wiped my tears. "You made your decision and it's time for me to allow the Jaws of Life to get ahold of you. I did my best with you and now I'm done. I wish you the best. Come on, I'll walk you out."

My father took me by the hand and walked me outside to the porch. He stood in front of me and kissed me on the forehead like he did all my life.

"I love you, Leilani, and don't you forget it. I wish you the best in life. Goodbye."

And just like that, he walked away from me and closed the door. I turned around and faced the driveway. Coy was sitting in the car waiting on me. I was an emotional mess and it felt like my life had just come to an end. I stepped from the porch and walked across the grass.

All of a sudden, my legs became wobbly and I felt weak, but I knew I had to keep on pushing. I took a few more steps before my legs finally decided to give out on me. I landed flat on my knees and stared straight up into the sky.

"God, please help me. I don't know what to do," I shouted, followed by the most gut-wrenching, horrific scream to ever leave my lungs.

Chapter 8

Five months later

Leilani

"Keep that ass spread open." Coy smacked me on my ass hard as *fuck, while hitting me from the back.*
Whap!

"Ah. Ah. I'm trying, but it hurts too bad!" I whined, swearing I was about to pass out. This fool must've forgot I was seven months pregnant with our son and this big ass stomach was in the way. The baby was already killing my bladder and the way he was rough housing my ass, made me think he was trying to do the same shit.

"Stop whining all the time and do what I tell you to do." He snatched my free hand and placed it back on my butt. "Hold it open, so I can beat the fuck out this pussy and I ain't stoppin' 'til you do it right," he growled.

Coy ignored my cries, lifted my leg onto the dresser and continued to pound on the box. Under normal circumstances, I wouldn't mind having rough sex, even though I didn't like it but damn, a bitch stomach was already hurting.

"Just slow down a little, please," I whimpered, damn near out of breath.
Whap!

He smacked me on the ass again. "Throw it back."

At that point, I had no choice but to do what he said, in order for this to be over with as quick as possible. Twirling my hips, I threw it back, while biting down on my lip from this excruciating pain.

"Hmm," I moaned. "Ooh."

I still hadn't got used to the immense size of his penis or the way he handled me so roughly. Sex was gentle with him on a whim.

"Ooh, this pussy so tight and hot, shit." He grunted, while grabbing a handful of my cheeks and squeezing them tight. "Pregnant pussy is the best." Coy was moaning and grunting like crazy. "I'm 'bouta nut. I'm 'bouta nut all in this pussy." Placing his fingers on my clitoris, he rubbed it aggressively, but it felt so good to me. It turned me on whenever he rubbed her, giving me mixed emotions about the pain I was feeling.

"Cum wit' me. Cream all over this dick for daddy. I'm ya' daddy now." He slapped my ass again.

"Mm. Mm. I am."

I closed my eyes and waited on him to finish fucking the air out my body, leaving me deflated. Suddenly, his hand was around my throat tight like a vice grip and he was pulling me towards him. This man was really trying to break my neck or give me whiplash or some shit. His grunts grew louder and louder, as I clenched my vagina muscles tightly around the base of his dick, like I was trying to pull the skin off of it.

"Squeeze that dick just like that."

He was taking too long to nut and I was ready to lay down. Every thrust was harder than the one before. Each time he drew back and slammed his pelvis against my ass, I could feel my stomach getting tighter and tighter. It felt like I was about to go into labor at any moment.

"Ooh. Ooh," I whimpered like a baby until he started to slow down.

"Shit. Shit. Don't move. Be still," Coy whispered, while taking slow strokes until he stopped completely. When I felt him pull his dick out, I was relieved and so was my kitty. I eased my numb leg off the dresser slowly. She was throbbing hard. As bad as I wanted to take a shower, the pain in my legs wouldn't allow me to stand up. So, that would have to wait until I recuperated for a few hours.

My legs felt wobbly when I took the first few steps, losing my balance in the process. Coy grabbed me around my waist to keep me from falling.

"Baby, you okay?" he panicked. I could tell he was nervous by the way he was constantly blinking and looking into my eyes.

"My legs feel weak."

He lifted me off the floor, taking me into his arms and carried me over to the bed. Then, he placed me onto the bed gently and pulled the blanket over my cold, naked body and sat down beside me. Coy rubbed my head and kissed me on the lips.

"My bad, baby. I guess I was a little too aggressive for you, but you know how I get sometimes. You need me to get you something to drink?"

"Yes." I nodded my head up and down.

"Okay. I'll be right back."

I stared at him with pure seduction and this huge grin on my face, as he walked out the room. My man was fine and dripping in chocolate just the way I liked it. His body was ripped and covered in tatts, all five feet eleven inches of it. Nothing else felt better than going to sleep and waking up next to him.

Coy used to play football at Dillard High School and he was good at it, but I guess it wasn't meant for him to go pro. During his senior year, he tore his ACL. Although he had treatment, he didn't fully recover from it, so he had to give it up for good.

It wasn't long before he returned with a bottle of water, placing it in my hand. "I opened it for you. Drink this and lay down for a few."

"I am."

"I'll be on the patio if you need me."

"Okay."

"I love you, Leilani, and I mean that. It's me and you against the world, baby."

"I love you too." Coy grabbed his cellphone from the dresser and walked out the room.

My mouth was dry as hell, so I turned the bottle up to my lips and took a very long gulp of it. When I finally released it, half of it was gone, so I sat it next to me in the bed. "Damn, we was thirsty."

I giggled, while rubbing my stomach. Anytime I would drink anything cold, the baby would kick constantly. "I wish you would've started kicking when your daddy was digging up in me and giving you shaken baby syndrome."

It was time for me to take a nap, so I laid down and cuddled up with my body pillow. I couldn't believe that after five months had passed, I still hadn't spoken to my father. As promised, he took away everything he said he would, including taking his name off of my car. The one thing he didn't do was take the thirty thousand dollars out of my savings account that he started when I was a baby. Every time I tried calling him, he would send me to voicemail and that shit hurt me to the core.

Leonard Jordan was everything to me. My world, my provider, my protector, the first man I ever loved and I was broken at how he abandoned me when I needed him the most. Tears dropped onto my pillow heavily, as my heart yearned for his forgiveness.

One day soon, I would go and see him and beg for him to come back into my life. This separation anxiety was going to be the death of me. I couldn't live without him, because I'd never done it before. Since the day I was born, he had been in my life and I needed him back if I wanted to keep my insanity.

* * *

After a much-needed nap, Coy and I went to the corner store on 55th Avenue, right around the corner from our apartment in Deepside to get me some snacks. This little boy inside of me had me feenin' for a hot sausage and salt and vinegar chips like crazy. Just as he pulled into a parking spot, his phone started to ring, but he didn't answer it. That made me curious as to who was calling. Tilting my head to the side, I asked, "Are you going to answer your phone?"

"Stop trippin' and go in there and get what you gon' get." He sat the phone face down in his lap like that was going to make me go away. My eyes locked on his phone. "It's a lick, damn."

"Answer the phone, Coy, and I'm not playing with you. What the fuck you hiding?" In my heart, I knew it was his ex, so I took a deep breath and tried fighting back the tears that so desperately wanted to fall. "I know it's your ex and that's why you don't want to answer. I should've listened to my daddy."

Coy looked over at me and his ass looked like the devil himself. Hearing me mention my father pissed him off, 'cause he never got over the fact that he pulled that gun out on him.

"What the fuck did you just say?" he yelled, causing my heart to skip a beat.

"Don't worry about it. Tend to your phone call and the bitch that's calling you." I placed my hand on the handle to open the door, but he snatched me by the collar and pulled me towards him.

"I'm tellin' you right now to be careful how you talk to me." His grip grew tighter, cutting off my air supply. Grabbing my collar from the front, I pulled it in an effort to free my lungs. "I don't want to hear shit 'bout yo' daddy. He don't fuck wit' chu, so I'm all you got and you will respect me."

When he finally let me go, I hungrily gasped for air and rubbed my neck where my shirt was cutting off the circulation and digging into my skin. His phone rang again, but this time he picked up.

"What the fuck you keep blowin' my shit up for? I'm wit' my girl," he snapped. When I looked at him, he put it on speaker.

"I don't give a fuck who you with." she paused for a second. "You so fuckin' rude, witcho ugly ass. Bring me a ounce," the girl screamed into the phone, then she hung up.

Coy sat the phone back in his lap face down and looked over at me. "Happy now?"

I got out the car and went inside the store. That didn't prove shit to me, so I looked down at my watch to see what time it was 'cause as soon as I got my hands on his phone, I was gone find out who that was.

Standing in front of the soda cooler, I was undecided on what I wanted to drink, due to my taste buds being all over the place.

"Hey beautiful, where yo' man at?" a voice from behind me whispered.

Rolling my eyes, I was disgusted at the fact he was so close to me in the first place. I grabbed a ginger-ale and when I turned around, a huge smile spread across my lips.

"Oh, my goodness, Dontae. It's been so long since I saw you." He reached down and gave me a hug. We had dated my freshman year when he was a junior, but decided it was best that we remained friends. After he graduated, we lost contact with one another. He was the one that got away, since my parents actually liked him.

"I went to the Navy after graduation and now I'm back for a little while to help the recruitment center in Lauderdale Lakes." He rubbed my stomach. "Who's the lucky man that pulled you away from your daddy?"

"It's a long story." I put my hand on his arm. "But hopefully, I get to see you before you leave. This is a nice jacket, but it's not cold enough for that yet." I admired his red Ducati jacket.

"I wear this when I ride my motorcycle." Dontae licked his thick full lips and it made me a little wet, thinking of what he could do to me. "Give me your number so we can meet up." He pulled out his iPhone and I programmed my number, then handed it back.

"So, this what's taking you so long? You in here flirting wit' another nigga, while I'm sitting outside?" Coy looked just as stupid as he sounded.

Dontae looked at me before he turned to face the man behind the noise. He stood a little over six feet, so he had to look down at Coy, sizing him up.

"It's nothing like that. We went to school together." I attempted to diffuse the situation, but Coy wasn't listening to me.

"Bruh, chill, it ain't nothing like that. I'm just speaking to an old friend." Dontae spoke up with that baritone voice I loved even back in school. I see a lot hadn't changed.

"Bruh, stay out of this when I'm talking to my girl, 'cause she ain't got no business talkin' to nan nigga." He looked past Dontae and looked me in the eyes. "Let's go."

"Aye, you need to chill out, for real." Dontae tried coming to my defense, but I stopped him because I still had to go home to that fool.

"Dontae, it's okay. It was nice seeing you. Take care." I walked off and went to pay for my stuff. It was so embarrassing to be checked by your man in front of a crowd of people. I tossed a five-dollar-bill on the counter and walked out, without getting my change.

As soon as we got in the car, he couldn't wait to start up more drama. "That's what we do now? Flirt with other niggas and shit?"

I was so sick of his shit already. "Whatever!" Putting my hand up to him, so he could talk to it, I was over the bullshit-ass accusations. His head was hard as a rock and there was no getting through to him. "Think what you want. I don't care."

Coy grabbed me by the hand and bent it backwards, making me scream out to God and anyone else who could hear me. "You don't care, huh? I'll break every one of these muthafuckas 'cause they ain't pregnant."

Tears surfaced in my eyes and I could feel the heat take over my body. The pain was unbearable and I could feel my hand becoming numb. "Coy, please stop. Please, you're hurting me," I begged repeatedly. "Stop."

On top of bending my fingers, he had the nerve to apply more pressure by squeezing it. I just knew I would pass out at any moment.

"I'm sorry," My voice was so low, but he could hear me since the radio wasn't on.

"Say that again, but a little bit louder." He was getting a kick out of me being at his mercy.

"I'm sorry. I won't do it again. I promise." Coy dropped my hand and it hit the middle console on the way down. It was aching so bad, I could barely move it.

"You better not or it's gon' be a lot worse next time and I'm dead ass serious 'bout that."

We finally made it home and that was the longest five minutes in human history. Instead of parking, he pulled up in front of our building and let me out.

"Go in the house. I'll be back in a few." I ignored him and slammed the car door behind me.

All I wanted to do was get away from him, but I knew he would only come looking for me. And, it wasn't like I had a place to go. If I knew then what I knew now, I would've walked away from Coy and chosen my daddy. Now I was stuck, living in hell with a man who didn't know if he wanted to love me, hate me, fuck me or fight me. I was truly living proof of Eve's song, "Love is blind."

Chapter 9

Coy

As I headed down Oakland Park to bust my lick, it gave me some time to reflect on my relationship with Leilani. The truth was, I love shorty with every fiber in my body and there ain't nothing I wouldn't do for her. My problem was I wasn't good at expressing my feelings and I didn't know how to treat her like the queen she is. She deserved to be happy and not go through all of the bullshit I had taken her through. I can admit I was selfish, jealous and I had a bad temper I couldn't control at times. That's just who I was. I wanted to change for her and give her a little freedom, but I was afraid of losing her. I knew for a fact that intimidation had the ability to make any female stay, because she would be too afraid to leave. I witnessed that shit with a friend of mine, and him and his lady was still together.

Growing up, I didn't have that mother figure I needed to nurture, love or teach me how to love a woman. The bitch that birthed me and pushed me out her nasty, corroded, alcoholic pussy wasn't there for me. All she cared about was getting drunk and fucked by every Tom, Dick and Harry. I had so many uncles, I lost count. A few of the steady boyfriends she did have wasn't shit, 'cause all they did was lay up and drink Mad Dog 20/20 on the daily. Majority of their sorry asses didn't work and the ones who did were even worse. They felt like they ran shit because she depended on them. Then, when they were good and drunk, they would fist fight all the time. I could recount every single incident that left her with a black eye, busted lip and a bloody nose. Violence was like second nature in that house and it seemed natural to kick your woman's ass from time to time, especially when she got out of line.

That bitch didn't care if I ate, took a bath or went to school. If alcohol or dick wasn't involved, she didn't give a flying fuck. For the life of me I couldn't understand why social services never picked my ass up. I guess they didn't give a fuck either. So, it was her fault I don't know how to love a woman properly.

When I came up to the light on 21st Avenue, I realized I almost missed my turn. Hooking a quick right, I slid onto the road, continuing my journey. Ten minutes later, I was in Lauderdale Manors, pulling up to my destination. Just as I was about to make a phone call, the front door swung open and out came Crystal. She came right to the passenger side, opened the door and flopped down next to me.

"Next time I call you, miss me with that attitude and unnecessary shit. Like I'm getting on your nerves and shit." Crystal was as ratchet as they came. This heffa rolled her eyes and neck at least twenty times. "If you too good for my money, just let me know and I'll cop from somebody else."

All I could do was laugh at the shit, 'cause it was pointless in gettin' upset with her. "Man, gone wit' all that bullshit." I passed her the bag of loud she asked for. "You don't even pay for the shit, so hush."

"Dead-ass. You answered the phone like I was calling for dick or some shit." Crystal opened the bag and inhaled the contents. "Talkin' 'bout you wit' yo girl. Like nigga, I don't give a fuck about that. You better be glad I'm talking to you after that shit you pulled at your apartment."

"Yo' ass crazy, man."

Crystal and I started messing around a while back. We wasn't exclusive, but shit still got crazy. She was five years older than me, even though she didn't act like it. That was when I met Leilani. After finding out she was a virgin, I doubled back and slept with Crystal, making shit worse.

"Whateva!" She smiled and waved the bag. "I'm about to get high as fuck, drunk as fuck, watch Pornhub and cum hard as fuck."

Crystal stuck two of her fingers in her mouth and sucked on them slowly. Shoving them in and out her mouth, she made the sexiest slurping sounds. My dick jumped in my pants, watching her freaky ass. She was what you would call a true head hunter and deep-throating dick was what she did best. Leilani didn't suck dick, so I was trying to get her comfortable enough to do it, to keep me from letting my ex suck my shit.

Pulling her fingers out her mouth, she made a slow, yet seductive trail down to her breasts. Her perky nipples were hard as hell, poking through her tank top. Using her index finger, she traced a perfect circle around them, then pulled on them gently. My mouth watered at the thought of sucking on them one by one. If I didn't leave now, I would be in her bed doing shit I had no business doing.

"Crystal, I gotta go." I said, finally finding the strength to say what was on my conscience.

"Don't you wanna fuck me, Coy?" Her moans were turning me on, but I was trying my best not to break.

"Nah, I gotta get back to the house and you just said you wasn't calling for dick." This girl was really carrying on, but I couldn't stop watching. Once she finished playing with her nipples, she slipped one of her hands inside her shorts. That hand was going to work full-circle on her clit.

"Ah. Ah. Coy, fuck me, please. Don't you see what you do to me?" She purred like a baby cougar. "I want you to make my pussy squirt."

"Come on, Crystal." This broad was gone make me snatch her up out my ride shortly if she didn't stop.

Suddenly, she stopped, then eased over to the driver seat grabbed my dick through my gym shorts and jerked it slowly. "I know that little girl don't fuck you like I do."

Crystal leaned in closer to me and licked my earlobe. "Come in the house and let me swallow all this dick." She knew that was my spot. My blood was boiling and my dick was throbbing. I was ready to fuck, so I turned my car engine off and pulled the keys from the ignition.

"Ten minutes and that's it." I opened up the car door and got out, so did Crystal. The sound of a motorcycle caught my attention as it hit the corner. It slowed down a little, looking in my direction for a few seconds before picking up speed once again.

"Um, let's go inside." Crystal grabbed my arm and pulled me towards her.

"Come on." Grabbing my phone from the seat, I stepped back and closed the door. "Who in here?"

"Nobody." She turned around and headed towards the door.

"Where them bad-ass kids at?" Crystal had four girls and three of them were some demon seeds, even her three-year-old daughter was terrible. The youngest, Jayla, only got a pass because she was still a baby. I'm certain that would change once she started walking.

"They wit' my mama."

Crystal was thick as fuck and her body was still tight after she pushed those babies out. My eyes were glued to her ass and thighs in the booty shorts she was wearing. That's what made it so hard for me to say no. When we got inside, she secured the locks on the door. I found me a spot on the couch and got comfortable. Walking over slowly, she unbuckled her shorts and eased them down to her ankles, before stepping out of them. Her neatly shaved peach was pretty with plump lips. It looked like a monkey knuckle down there. I was so turned on. I pulled my pipe from my gym shorts and jacked his ass slowly, as my eyes locked in on hers.

"Nah, let me handle that for you." She stood in between my legs and dropped to her knees, taking my shit from my hands.

Her palms were soft and small, making my shit look enormous in her hands. Stroking it up and down, she licked the tip of my head before placing her lips on it and eased it into her mouth. I swear, I felt a tingle down my spine. With my cellphone in my hand, I unlocked the screen and turned on the camera. She was a freak like that and didn't mind if I recorded her. We did that a lot when we were together.

"Yeah." I stretched that word to death. "Suck that dick just like that." I put my left hand on her head and pushed it down until I could feel the back of her throat. "That's right, don't gag, take that shit."

This girl was a certified head doctor and those were straight facts. My camera froze. The incoming call fucked up my video.

"Fuck!" To say I was annoyed was an understatement. Leilani knew when to fuck some shit up. That muthafucka would fuck up a wet dream with no remorse. I sent her ass to voicemail and resumed my video.

Crystal popped my dick out her mouth and licked the pre-cum from her lips. "Ignore her."

"Speak into the mic." I laughed. That was all I needed to say, before she went back to work without taking her eyes off me. She was confident and that made it easy for her to hold eye contact every time she sucked me up. The glitter lip gloss on her lips was poppin' and it looked good on camera.

Seeing her slick-ass mouth full of meat had me weak and I felt vulnerable to her. Those lips were soft and the inside was warm and wet. My toes were balled up inside my Nikes and I couldn't help but to close my eyes and enjoy this fire head. It made a nigga feel like he was in outer space or some shit. As soon as I got into it, those muthafuckas shot open like I was beaming as soon as I heard my phone ring once again.

"Dammit, girl. What the fuck you keep calling me for?" I snapped and slapped Crystal across the head. "Be quiet, 'cause you like to be messy and shit."

She ignored me and started making slurping sounds. "Stop playin', 'cause I'm 'bouta answer the phone." The noise came to a halt immediately.

"What's up?" I answered coolly.

"Where are you?" Leilani's voice cracked. It sounded as if she was crying.

"About to come. Home. What's going on?"

"My stomach is killing me and I think I need to go to the hospital. This don't feel right, Coy, and I'm scared."

"I'll..." I had to pause 'cause Crystal was humming on my piece hard and I could feel myself about to bust.

"You'll what?" Leilani screamed.

A nigga had to catch his breath. "Be there shortly, just hang tight."

"I'm spotting, come now before we lose the baby," she screamed hysterically.

"A'ight. I'm on my way now."

"Right now," she replied before I hung up the phone.

Once the phone was completely hung up, I tossed the phone to the side and grabbed her head and fucked her mouth hardcore style. That wasn't good enough though, so I snatched her up by the hair in order for me to stand up. I had been watching porn and I was ready to act some of that shit out. Crystal was still on her knees, but she allowed her butt to rest on her feet, while she waited on me to take off my shorts and boxers.

"Hurry up," she whined, while trying to make her long hair weave lay down. It was tamed before I got ahold of it. Now, it was a little tangled at the top, but I didn't care cause I was about to mess it up again.

When I stepped in front of her, I grabbed her hair and wrapped it around my hand twice. My hand was on my piece, which was still hard as ever, so I pulled her head back and smacked her across the lips with my shit several times. Crystal stuck her tongue out and licked it first, before I shoved every inch down her throat. I swear, I felt like it was where I belonged.

Closing my eyes, I focused on busting a nut so I could get out of there and check on my unborn child. If something was to happen to her, while I was out trying to get some pussy, I would never forgive myself. Thrusting my hips back and forward, I stabbed the back of her throat repeatedly. When I opened my eyes and looked down in her face, those light brown eyes could barely stay open. The way she gagged sounded like her ass was about to throw up, but I didn't let that deter me from getting mine.

That wonderful tingling sensation I had been waiting on had surfaced and I could feel my knees buckle. I was ready to release that pressure. Pulling my dick from her locked jaws, I used the other hand to pull her head back.

"Hold your mouth open." Squeezing the shaft, I stroked it back and forward until my thick, white nut oozed from the tip and dropped into her mouth. "Ah. Ah. Ss. Ah. Shit, girl." The more I stroked it, the more came out and when I was finally finished, I shook it then rubbed it across her lips, smearing it all over her face.

"Damn, that was good." I let my limp homie fall from my hands then I took a step back.

"Did you just really give me a facial?" Crystal wiped my babies off her face with the shirt she was wearing.

There was no need in answering, so I walked off in the direction of the bathroom. I had to get home fast and see what was going on with my baby. Taking a quick piss, I grabbed the wipes from the sink and cleaned myself off, then tossed them into the trash. By the time I was walking out the bathroom, Crystal was making her way towards me, with this mean mug on her face.

"Don't be mad at me." She was still naked from the waist down, so I palmed her soft ass and squeezed it. "I promise, I'll make it up to you."

"What now?" Rolling her eyes and sucking her teeth.

"I have an emergency, so I gotta take a rain check." Leaning towards her, I kissed her on the cheek. "Keep it tight for me, a'ight?" I grinned while smacking her on the ass.

"Yeah, whatever." Crystal spun on her heels and went back into the living room and snatched her shorts up off the floor. "You think you so slick, but it's cool, tho."

"Man, gone with all that, you see she was calling me back to back. I have to take her to the hospital and make sure my son okay. You somebody mama, so you know what it is." I didn't have time to argue with her, so instead I put my boxers and shorts back on, grabbed my cellphone and went to the door.

Unlocking both knobs, I froze, then looked over my shoulder. "I need to holla at you about some business, so I'll be back."

"Yeah." She rolled them eyes again.

"Fix ya face and stop whining. You gone get the dick and I promise to knock that period on when I hit it." That always made her feel better, because she knew I would deliver on my promise.

"When are you going to tell her?" Crystal folded her arms across her chest, leaning back on her heels with this devious look on her face.

"Crystal, didn't we talk about this already? I told you that I will tell her soon." This girl was really about to stress me clean the fuck out with all this extra shit.

"Yeah, but I don't know how long you expect me to keep this a secret. It's been months now and still nothing. Make me think you just trying to drag this shit out as long as you can."

"Now is not a good time. She going through a lot right now. When she have the baby, I'll tell her." The truth was, I didn't want to tell her and if I could keep this secret forever, then I would.

"I'm going through shit too, but that doesn't matter to you. All you care about is your precious Leilani."

Crystal dropped her hands to the side and took two steps towards me. "You have thirty days to tell her or I will do it myself. I'm not about to just sit around in silence, while you live this double life. I almost busted you, 'cause I know you had me on speaker and that she was right there beside you. Treating me like a lick and shit."

Threats were something that I didn't take lightly and Crystal must've forgot that I kicked ass on the regular. If no one knew my get down, she did and right now she was testing my gangster. Turning away from the door, I took a few steps towards her until I was in her face. This bitch needed to feel what the fuck I was about to say.

"So, you trying to hand down ultimatums now?" My jaw was clenched so tight, I felt myself mumbling. "You know what it is and what it was. I didn't force you to do shit, that was all you."

Crystal rolled her eyes, then sucked her teeth. "Boy bye, like this all my fault. Get the fuck outta here with that bullshit."

She knew I hated that shit, but I had been letting her slide with a lot of shit for a while now. Not today though, 'cause I was putting an end to all that shit. I grabbed her ass by the jaw and locked down on it with a tight squeeze. Since I was taller than her, I lifted her head, raising her up on her tippy toes. We needed eye contact, so she could get this knowledge and let it marinate.

"Let me tell yo' ass something. I run this shit and what I say goes. I decide when she finds out. Leilani is my problem, not yours and you better watch that slick talk, before I knock out yo' front teeth."

Crystal's eyes were glassy when she stared at me. I could feel where she was coming from, but she needed to get it through her head that there was only one captain of the ship and that was me. No woman was gone tell me what to do, when to do it or how to do it. I was the man and they were gonna respect me, or get beat the fuck down. If a female acted like a man, then they needed to be treated like one.

"When I decide the time is right, you will know but until then, sit here, take care of your kids and keep quiet, 'cause that's what I pay you for right?" I shook my head up and down.

She closed her eyes and that made me feel like she was tuning a nigga out, so I applied more pressure, sinking her gums between her teeth. Her eyelids fluttered and I knew she was in pain.

"Open your eyes when I talk to you." She didn't hesitate on popping them bitches back open. "I pay you to be quiet, right?" She nodded her head yes. "I pay all the bills in this bitch, right?" She nodded her head once more. "And most importantly, I call the shots right?"

After the final head nod, I released her from my grip, then placed my lips on hers and stuck my tongue in her mouth. There was no passion in that kiss whatsoever and I knew she didn't want to kiss me after that, but I didn't care. It was my way or the Lord's way. I knew for a fact she didn't want it his way, 'cause that meant I would send her ass to meet our savior behind those pearly gates.

Using my free hand, I put my hand between her legs and massaged her fatty with my fingers. The pattern in her breathing changed and her body suddenly became relaxed. Knowing I won her over just like that was funny as fuck. I ended our kiss abruptly, then gently wiped the saliva from her lips, before pecking them for the last time.

"I gotta go, but I'll be back to tuck you in tonight. Keep that shit warm for daddy and have on some boy shorts when I get back."

And like a boss I walked off, leaving her standing in her place, yearning and anxiously awaiting my return. When I stepped onto the porch, I closed the door behind me and jogged to my car before Leilani started back blowing my shit up.

Chapter 10

Leilani

"Do you know his ass still not here?" My voice was loud and I could feel every throat muscle move as I talked on the phone.

It had been all of twenty minutes since I called Coy to come and he still hadn't walked his black ass in the door yet. My blood was boiling and I wanted to curse him out so bad for trying me like I was some stupid ass, naïve ass bitch.

"I'm sorry, Leilani, maybe I shouldn't have said anything. That's my fault." Dontae tried taking the blame for what Coy's dog ass was doing to me. "I just felt that as a friend, it was my responsibility to tell you the truth. It was a reason I took that street today, so take that as a sign."

Of course, I didn't blame him, but my emotions were straddling the fence on if I really wanted to know the truth. My woman's intuition told me he wasn't being faithful to me. I just didn't want to hear it, and definitely not from another man. All this did was confirm what I already knew, but this time I knew where the bitch lived and who it was. His ex-girlfriend, Crystal. The one he claimed he wasn't fucking with no more.

I let out a long, painful sigh before I responded. "It's not your fault. This is all on me and I had a feeling he was cheating, but I just couldn't prove it."

As I leaned forward on the edge of the bed, I massaged my forehead and temple, because I could feel a headache coming on. "I feel so stupid for throwing my life away. I could've been at Harvard, living the college life right now, but no, my dumb ass threw it all away on the strength of a nigga that probably don't love me."

The minute Dontae told me he saw Coy at a girl house, my world felt like it had been knocked off the earth's axis.

"Damn, Leilani, it's fucked up how you have to go through this while you pregnant."

I appreciated his sympathy, but nothing was going to stop the constant pang in my heart. "You just don't understand what I'm going through. My father has cut me off completely and now I'm all alone. I'm surprised he let me keep the car."

"You're not alone, Leilani." Dontae paused for a bit, then exhaled. "You have me and I'll be here for you. I promise."

"Thanks, Dontae, I appreciate that. He has run everybody in my life away from me and he's happy about that. All he says is he's all I got. He so intimidating." I moved further back onto the bed and positioned myself on my side.

"Well, he don't intimidate me and he can't make me stop talking to you." Dontae chuckled. "These hands are certified."

I laughed also. Just the thought of him defending me was cute. "I do not want y'all fighting and besides..." The sound of the front door caught me off guard. "Dontae, I gotta go, he's here."

I didn't give him a chance to respond, because I hung that phone up so fast and tossed it underneath my arm. Rocking my body, I pretended to be in so much pain. My eyes were already red from me crying while I was talking on the phone with Coy, after hearing the news. My heart was racing with anticipation, like I was the one cheating. It wasn't like we were in a mansion, so I don't know why it was taking him so long to get in the room. Shortly after, I heard the bathroom door close and water running.

A single tear slipped from my eye, dripping onto the pillow. In my heart, I knew he fucked that girl, 'cause why else would he come in and go straight to the bathroom, instead of checking on me? It made my stomach hurt, just wondering about the things he did to her while he was there. *If he fucked her or made love to her the same way he does with me? Did she suck his dick and did he give her head? Or, if he even used a condom?* My body jerked as I laid in bed weeping, because I didn't understand how he could continue to hurt me physically, mentally and emotionally. It made me wonder if he did it because I wasn't experienced or freaky, like he encouraged me to be.

The bathroom door finally opened and I could hear his heavy footsteps coming into the room. "Boo, you okay?" He sat down beside me, placing his hand on my stomach. "Is the baby okay?" I shrugged my shoulders, but I didn't open my mouth. "You still wanna go to the hospital?" I nodded my head up and down.

Coy got up from the bed and I could feel his hands on my legs. "Come on, let's go."

"Help me up." I sniffled.

Grabbing my legs, he pulled them to the edge of the bed, allowing them to dangle. "Roll over."

I did what he told me to do and rolled onto my back. He looked into my eyes, but he quickly looked away. That right there told me he was guilty. My dad taught me how to pay attention to body language and eye contact, so I could easily pick up on a lie.

Coy grabbed me by the arms and pulled me up. I assisted so he wouldn't be lifting dead weight. "Damn yo' ass heavy." He took a few deep breaths and put his hand on his chest, like his ass was really out of oxygen.

I swear, I wanted to slap that stupid smirk off his face. "Do you have to be an insensitive, pompous jackass all the time? I mean damn this is your baby I'm carrying."

The smirk he had on his face quickly disappeared and his eyes widened with feigned shock, while staring at me. Sad part about it is that he knew my statement was factual, but here he was, acting all surprised with his emotionless ass. Coy brought his hand from his side and backhanded me with the quickness.

Whap!

My head snapped back and I stumbled backwards, hitting my heel on the side of the wooden frame.

"Ouch!" The pain in my foot and face were stinging simultaneously. I didn't know which one to tend to first, but my reflexes brought my hand to my face. "Why you keep hitting on me?"

"Learn how to stay in your place. You talk too fuckin' much." Coy covered my face with the palm of his hand and mushed me. "You better be lucky we going to the hospital, 'cause

I'll beat ya' ass right now," he screamed with his finger pointed in my face.

I knew not to say anything else, so I dropped my head and focused on my fat feet that had sunken into the soft, beige carpet. When he walked away, I left the spot I was standing in and slipped on my slides that were beside the bed. On my way out the bedroom, I went inside the bathroom and stood in front of the mirror. My hands shook as I placed my hand on the light switch, fearing I had a bruise on my face. When I flicked it on, I gazed into the mirror and was surprised that my butterscotch skin was still the same tone.

"What the fuck you doing in there? Let's go, goddamit," Coy yelled, startling me.

Not wanting to cause any more problems, I grabbed my rag from the towel rack, wet it and washed my face quickly. Once I was finished, I turned off the light and rushed through the door, bumping into him.

"What the fuck you doing?" His eyes glared down on me, like he wanted to slap me again.

"I was washing my face." Without another word, he turned on his heels and went to the front door.

***

The emergency room wasn't as bad as I expected it to be. There were about four people in the waiting room, but who knew what awaited me in the back. Out of all places, he brought me to the private hospital in Plantation, instead of where I wanted to go. When I mentioned it, he had a fit about not wanting to drive far and this was closer to the house.

The sound of the microphone caught my attention. "Leilani Jordan, come to triage please. Leilani Jordan to triage."

Coy got up and helped me out my seat. Standing on my feet, I adjusted my shirt before walking off. There was a nurse sitting down in a chair when we walked in. She looked up with this huge smile on her face.

"Have a seat right here, mommy." I walked over and took a seat across from her. "I'm going to check your vital signs and ask you a series of questions, okay?"

"Yes, ma'am."

The nurse checked my vital signs quickly, then moved on to the questionnaire. "Do you have any relevant past medical history? Such as cystic fibrosis, thyroid disease, high blood pressure?" She looked up for confirmation.

"No, ma'am."

"Where is the pain located? Point to it for me."

There was really no pain. I only lied so Coy could come home. I placed my hand at the bottom of my stomach. "Right here."

"On a scale of one to ten, how would you rate your pain?"

"Um. I would say an eight." My eyes glanced up at Coy to see what he was doing. Of course, he was standing there with this absent look on his face, like there was someplace else he would rather be. All I could do was shake my head and place my attention back on the nurse.

"Would you consider that pain to be sharp, burning, dull, aching or cramping?"

"Cramping." I rubbed my stomach in a circular motion to make it seem like it was hurting at that moment.

"How frequent is it, irregular or continuous?"

"Continuous."

"How about the severity? Is it mild, moderate or severe?"

"Moderate."

The nurse rambled off a dozen more questions, nothing was excluded. I swear, it felt like I was taking a midterm on my health. All I wanted to do was get in this back room and get this bogus report, so I could go home.

"Okay and final question. I know you're tired of responding." She smiled.

"It's a lot, but I'm okay," I replied, smiling back at her.

"What is your marital status? Single, married, divorced or separated."

"Single."

"Oh, you single now?" Coy jumped in, embarrassing the hell out of me once again. Then, he looked at the nurse. "She ain't no muthafuckin' single."

The nurse's brow creased, as she stood there with a blank look on her face. I knew she was just as confused as me.

"Um. Okay. It's really not that serious of a question, sir, it's for insurance purposes only." She turned her attention back to me. "I'm going to take you back to a room now, so the doctor can see you as quickly as possible."

"Okay."

The nurse got up from her seat and grabbed the clipboard. "Right this way."

Coy didn't help me from my seat this time, so I had to use both hands and push myself up as he stood there and watched. When I walked past him, I brushed against him intentionally, adding a little elbow to it. I loved him, but he could be really stupid at times. We walked through a set of double doors, then down a hallway, before hooking a left at the nurse's station. We ended up at a room that was off in the cut.

"Okay, so just go in here and get comfortable. The doctor will be with you in just a moment." The nurse looked at me with the saddest eyes and I knew she was concerned about me, thanks to foolio and his outburst.

"Thank you," I replied, trying to sound normal as possible.

"You're welcome."

The nurse closed the door, leaving me alone with the psychopath. I walked over to the bed and sat down on the edge.

Coy was standing in the middle of the floor, with his hands in his pockets, staring at me with the darkest eyes. It made me shiver all over. The look of death was in his eyes and he looked as if he wanted to hurt me badly.

"Leilani, you single?" His voice was low, yet stern.

"Coy that's a dumb question. We both know I'm not single."

"But, you didn't tell that to the nurse," he replied.

"Coy, stop tripping, it's not that serious." If looks could kill, I would be on my way to the morgue. "You act like boyfriend was on the list or something."

Coy took two giant steps and he was hovering over me with his fists balled up. "I look like a fuckin' joke to you?"

Intimidation was a bitch, because he had me shook all the way down to the bone. My heart was thumping so hard, I felt it in my throat. In my mind, I was praying he didn't hit me in this hospital. I tried my best to keep the tears underneath the surface.

"I didn't say that." My voice box trembled, trying to get those words out.

He bent down and got in my face. "I'm yo' man, right?" I shook my head with no hesitation. "No, open your mouth and answer me. I ain't deaf and yo' ass ain't mute. Dumb, but not mute."

"Yes," I muttered.

"Well, act like it. Next time a muthafucka ask you that question, you better get that shit right, or I'm a go in yo' shit wherever we at." He hit his chest with his fist. "Acknowledge me, goddamitt."

Coy backed up and placed both hands on his head. "Nah, you got me fucked up and I'm gon' teach you about trying me." He dropped his hands and bopped in place. "Oh yeah, you gon' learn tonight, you gon' feel this shit."

My bottom lip quivered. "No, please. I'm sorry. I won't do it again," I rambled.

"Oh, after this, I know you won't so I ain't worried about that."

The door opened and I was relieved, but to my surprise, it wasn't the doctor. It was the nurse from triage. "The doctor is with a patient, but he'll be right over." She looked at Coy, then back to me. "Are you okay?"

"Yes, ma'am. I'm fine." Deep down inside, I wanted to tell her what was going on so he could go to jail, but I had no place to go. The money in my savings couldn't be touched and I couldn't find a place, because I had no job. I was fucked. Instead, I forced a fake smile. "I'm good. Thanks for checking on me."

"Okay." The nurse closed the door. That lady knew I was in danger and I think she was trying to get me to indicate it without saying it. She had to think I was the dumbest bitch on the planet.

"That bitch think she slick and I wish you would say something to her ass, about what goes on in the privacy of our home."

"I didn't say anything."

"Come on. We leaving, or you stay and walk home when you done. I ain't staying in here."

Coy opened the door and I followed behind him like a lovesick puppy. This shit was crazy and I had never experienced no shit like this before. My daddy never put his hands on my mama like this.

As we walked through the corridor, I was certain that someone was going to say something to us. To be honest, I was hoping they would. Sadly, we made it back to the emergency room and outside to the parking lot. My legs were tired from trying to keep up with him. He was walking like a man on a mission. When we finally made it to the car, I was ready to sit down and get off my feet. He started the car up and pulled off.

"Coy, please don't beat me. I'm sorry." He faced forward and didn't acknowledge me at all, but I needed to know what to expect. "Are you going to beat me?"

We came up to a red light by the hospital exit and that was when he looked at me with the coldest eyes. It sent chills down my spine. "You did this, so whatever happens, just know that it's your fault and you brought this on yourself."

The light changed and he pressed down hard on the gas. My head hit the headrest. It was like he was in a hurry to beat my ass. I didn't do shit to warrant such a punishment. Folding my hands together, I closed my hands and said a silent prayer, begging God to let me endure whatever pain was about to be inflicted upon my body.

Chapter 11

Coy

My blood was boiling in the driver's seat as I flushed it past every car, doing sixty miles per hour. Sunrise Boulevard had fucked-up traffic, no matter what time you drove on it. I was anxious to put my foot in her ass for trying me like I'm a soft-ass, sucker-ass nigga. This bitch had me fucked up on every level, but I was gone show her who the boss and who she belonged to. I was her muthafuckin' daddy now and she needed to get that through her head. It was obvious that she forgot, but I was about to give that ass a reminder she would never forget.

When I crossed the bridge by the turnpike, rain started pouring down from nowhere blocking everything in front of me. I quickly turned on the windshield wipers and made a left on 56th Avenue. From there, it was a straight shot to the apartment. We were only three minutes away and I was catching every damn light. All that was doing is prolonging what I had planned for this ungrateful ass heifer sitting beside me. After the last light, I finally pulled into our complex and slid through the guard gate.

It was still pouring down when I parked the car. Under any other circumstances, I would've dropped her to the front, but she was gone walk in this rain with me. Killing the engine, I pulled the keys out the ignition and looked over at her. Leilani didn't move a muscle.

"Get out the car," I instructed her.

"It's raining."

"You scared of water now?" She sat there staring out the window like she didn't hear what the fuck I said. Catching her from behind, I banged her head against the window one good time.

Boom!

Leilani let out a painful scream and grabbed her head. I sat there and watched her as she rocked in her seat sobbing and holding her forehead.

"When I talk, you answer, simple. Now get out the car and don't make me repeat myself."

I waited on her to unbuckle her seatbelt before I opened my door and got out. When she closed the door, I triggered the alarm. The jack boys be out and about, but I wasn't worried about nobody touching my shit, 'cause these niggas knew what it was whenever they saw that candy-apple-red bubble Chevy with the twenty-six-inch rims on it. About my shit, I'll leave a nigga stankin' in some bushes around this bitch.

We had finally made it inside the apartment and it was show time. Leilani needed to learn her lesson about disrespecting a G. I locked us in and we went straight to the bedroom. Our clothing was soaked and sticking to our bodies, so I removed the shoes, shirt and pants I was wearing. Leilani took her time removing her pants. Her pace was much slower than mine and I knew it was because she wasn't aware of what was about to happen next. Suspense would drive a sane person crazy. The sound of the crying and sniffling was killing my ears. I was seconds away from giving her something to really cry about. I waited patiently until she stepped completely out of them. She then bent over to pick them up from the floor.

As she was coming up, I balled up my fist and punched her dead in the nose. Leilani's body flew backwards, crashing hard onto the bed.

"I told you about disrespecting me, but you just don't fuckin' listen. This shit could've been avoided if you knew your place as my woman."

Blood was gushing from her nostrils and when she rubbed her hand across her nose, she panicked once she observed her blood soaked shirt.

"You bust my nose." She was hollering and holding her nose with both hands.

"You damn right I did. Fuck you thought." I don't know who she thought she was hollering at.

I grabbed Leilani by the leg and punched her repeatedly in her thigh. *Bop! Bop! Bop!* Her ass was kicking, hollering and crying like a hit dog.

"You single, right?"

Bop!

"Answer me."

Bop!

"Who baby that is? That nigga, Dontae?"

Bop! Bop! Bop! Bop!

She couldn't utter a single word. Every blow I delivered took her breath away, and her sounds were becoming fainter by the second. The kicking had even subsided. That was the moment I stopped to look at the damage I had caused. "That'll teach you about testing my gangster. "Now stop all that crying shit and go take a bath. You getting blood on the sheets."

I went to the closet, got me a sweat suit and changed my clothes. Leilani was in the same spot. "I'm gone and yo' ass betta not go nowhere. As a matter of fact…" I paused, then looked around the room for her bag. When I spotted it I opened it up and fished around in it until I found her car keys and cellphone.

"I'm taking your phone and car keys to make sure you don't leave me. I'll be back after I finish this job."

Honestly, I was headed to Crystal's house to fuck some sense into her head, before she go running her mouth. I didn't need any of my business in the streets and certainly not before I told Leilani. That would be on my own terms.

***

The next day I was in beast mode, so I slid up on my uncle Duke at his crib. After spending the night with Crystal and knocking sense into her ass all night, I was ready to get on some gangster shit. This wood worked like magic on both of my chicks. That's how I'm able to pull Houdini's on they asses, but when they get out of pocket, that's when I kicked ass. The rule was simple, obey me and get good dick and gifts. Disobey me and get hard painful dick and these fists upside they muthafuckin' heads. Either way they fucked.

I left Crystal sprawled out, butt booty naked in bed, after ten hours of straight pound action. She'll be good for a while. My mind drifted onto Leilani and it hurt my heart on the real. My intention is not to damage shorty, 'cause I really do love her. I just didn't know how to treat her. So whenever I made it back home, I was gone make it up to her.

Duke moved the Cohiba he was puffing once he saw me cross the threshold of his living room. "What's shakin', nephew?"

I walked over and dapped him up before taking a seat diagonal of where he was seated. "Ready to get on my bullshit as soon as you give me the word."

He sat the cigar in the ashtray, folded his hands and placed them into his lap. "I want you to slide up on that nigga, Josh. He late on his payment."

"No problem. I'm on it." I grinned as I was rubbing my hands together. "That flaw-ass nigga act hard around his new crew, but he pussy in real life. I grew up with the man." Josh and I grew up in the same neighborhood. We went to the same schools and all, so of course we had a friendship. All that shit changed once I found out he smashed my chick. That created this beef between us.

"Collect my shit. Don't leave without it and if he ain't got it, take him out and whoever he with." Unc retrieved his cigar and leaned back in his seat.

"Consider it done." I stood up and dapped him once more. "I'm out. I'll get at cha later."

My uncle sold heavy dope back in the day, but all of that had changed when he did five years in prison. The minute he touched down, he was ready to jump back in the game head-first, but somebody else had that bitch on lock like fat feet in tube socks. A lot of his archnemeses were the suppliers, which made it impossible for him to get on. Seeing he was shit of luck, he came up with the idea of extorting the workers, since the bosses were untouchable. We ran down on a few of their soft asses at their homes, and laid down the threat of killing their loved ones, if they chose not to cooperate. I had no problems with leaving a nigga flat on his back, looking up at the ceiling of a church. This extortion shit was sweet though. It was like taking candy from a baby.

***

Later on that night, I was slumped down in my seat, sitting in the cut staking out Josh's house. It was dark as shit. None of the street lights were working, but that was better for me, since I would be sitting for a while. I wasn't leaving until I ran down on his square ass. I hated red niggas with a passion. Every last one I ran across was Charmin soft. Only weak ass punks would let another man take his cash and shit. I'd rather die like a man than live like a coward.

An hour had passed and I was still in position. By this time, my ass was yawning. Slanging dick day and night was like a job and I was tired as hell. A set of high beam headlights hit the street, blinding me in the process. I leaned my body closer to the door to position myself behind the steering wheel. Normally, I wouldn't drive Leilani's car, but I needed to be ducked off. As soon as night hit, I went over there and took the car without going upstairs to check on her.

Pulling my hoodie over my head, I grabbed my fo' fifth and eased out quietly. Josh was just getting out the car as I crept up slowly. The passenger door opened, so I paused and out stepped a female. She walked over to the driver's side where he was standing, grabbed his face and kissed him. Josh placed both hands on her ass and tongued her down, but I knew he wasn't hitting that right at all.

Finally, they brought that lovey-dovey shit to an end and went to the front door. I tiptoed behind them quietly. Josh stepped to the side and let shorty walk in first. Just as he was closing the door, I placed my hand on the knob, twisting it before he had the chance to lock it. Snatching the door open, I pointed the steel in his face and smiled.

"Well, if it ain't fuck boy, McCoy." Josh backed up and walked in, closing the door behind me. The bitch got one good look at me and squealed like a pig. "Shut up, bitch, and sitcho fine ass down while men talk."

"Just stay calm, baby. This will be over soon."

"Aww, look at you trying to keep your girl calm and you scared." The shit was hilarious to me. I looked over at his girl and winked. "Yeah, listen to your man. Sit over there and be cute and quiet."

Josh took a few more steps back with his chest puffed out like he was about to buck or some shit. "What the fuck you doing, Coy?"

"Nigga, you know why I'm here. So save that dumb act for yo' hoes when they catch you trickin' off with another ho." I bit down on my lip and looked him up and down. "Where the fuck is my uncle money?"

Fear stricken, his eyeballs expanded and sweat started to protrude from his forehead. "Man I told yo' uncle I needed more time. I don't have all the money yet. Shit moving slow right now." His voice trembled, as he spit out lie after lie.

I pulled the hammer back on my bitch, grinning like a maniac. He insulted my intelligence. "But, you had enough money to go out and buy a new Range Rover." His brow shifted. "Don't act surprised, nigga, I saw the paper tag. Seems to me like you sayin', fuck my uncle."

Feeling a bit confused, I scratched my head because I knew goddamn well we laid out the rules in the beginning. "How many times do I have to keep repeating myself? If you want to hustle in these streets, it's a price to pay. If you wanna cross the bridge, you gotta pay the toll. I keep saying the same shit over and over again. This shit ain't free, my nigga."

"Since when was extortion a part of the game?" he blurted out.

Josh looked me in the eyes like he meant that shit. To me, I felt like he was testing my authority, so I cocked my arm back and smacked his ass across the head with my heat. His body dropped to the floor with a loud thump!

Shorty screamed again, but she never moved from that spot she was sitting in. "Please don't hurt him, we have kids together. Josh, just give him whatever he wants so he can go."

"Ya' chick smarter than you and I think you should listen to her, 'cause I'm losing my patience."

Josh was on the floor with his hand over his freshly opened wound. When he looked up at me, I could see the blood running down the side of his face. Some had even gotten in his eyes. "Tell Duke I'll have it for him in one week. All of it."

"Nah, it don't work like that. We call the shots and you have exhausted your payment extension privileges. Pay up or get popped. The choice is yours, but in the meantime, I'ma teach you 'bout playin' with me." I kicked him a few times in his side, then stomped his head with my Timberland boot, immobilizing him. "Now, you think about what you wanna do, while I handle some business over here." I walked in the direction of his baby mama. From behind I could hear him groaning, but I couldn't make out what he was saying.

"Stand up and walk over to that table." She got up without hesitation to follow my instructions, unlike her disrespectful ass dude. I stood behind her sexy ass, admiring that fatty and that tight ass dress she was wearing. It looked like that shit was painted on. I glanced over at Josh and he was struggling to see what was going on. So, I winked at him, while squeezing her booty.

"Coy, that's the mother of my kids, dawg. Come on, don't do this. You can take anything you want."

"That's what I'm doing right now." I slid my hand underneath her dress and she tensed up. "I want this right here."

My hands slithered across her fat lips until my fingers grazed her clit. That thang was pulsating down there, so I rubbed it.

"Relax, shorty. This ain't shit you never done before. If you love this nigga, then you'll participate."

"I will," she moaned. My fingers were going to town and I could feel her juices on my fingertips. She was comfortable with my touch.

"Bend over and plant your hands on the table." I looked at Josh. "Boy, she obedient like a muthafucka too. You got a good one right here." I joked, while raising her dress, exposing those brown cheeks.

I smacked it hard and she didn't utter a word. My shit was on swole when I pulled it out. Josh nutted up and went to speaking Creole.

"Fuck l, pran zam l, li tire l." He mumbled over and over again.

I didn't understand shit he was saying and it didn't matter to me, but he was about to shut up with all that bullshit. My eyes were locked in on him when I slid my gun to the back of her head. That immediately made him close his mouth, but I needed him to remain that way.

Chapter 12

Coy

"Take these off and give 'em to me." I tugged on her thong and she slipped them off, placing them in my hand. My dick was still out, but I didn't care. I walked over to Josh and shoved her thong in his mouth. "Be quiet and if you say another word, I'll smoke her ass in front of you. Can't you see we busy over here?" I kicked him in the ribs before I walked off.

Now it was time to let him catch this live porno with me and his baby mama. Rubbing her clit once more, I checked to make sure she was still wet. My piece was aching and anxious in my hand. It was ready to pound some twat. It was nothing like having a live audience.

The tip was throbbing. I quickly glided it in between her lips, rubbing it against her opening. Shorty wiggled her hips like she was ready to take all this dick. Without warning, I pushed past her lips and shoved every inch into her slippery, warm tunnel, giving steady pumps.

"Ahhh," she shrieked. "Umm."

"Yeah, that's it." I grunted in excitement. "Throw it back to daddy." Shorty locked her pussy muscles on my ass and I almost hollered like a female. I could see Josh over there crying like a ho' nigga. "Josh. Whoo!" I lost my breath for a moment. "This that grade-A right here."

This girl wasn't about to fuck me like she was crazy, so I slowed down to get myself together. It was time to turn that around. Slipping my gun into my pocket, I placed both hands on her cheeks and spread them apart, then drilled that ass.

"Ah! Ah! Ooh! Ooh!" Shorty was all into it. She arched her back a little more and laid down flat on the table. Seeing her body squirm and booty bounce was my motivation.

My no-good ass looked at Josh. "Arghh!" Our noises were on one accord and it sounded like a dope-ass beat from Mannie

Fresh. "This how you beat up the pussy. I know you don't fuck her like this."

I was trying to beat her back in. The only thing that could be heard was grunting and skin slapping. I grabbed her by the hair, using my left hand and snatched her head back. With my right hand, I placed my hand on her shoulder to pin her in place and dig deep in them guts.

"Oww!" she cried. "Ooh! Ooh!" Her fuck faces was everything.

"I fuck you better than this nigga, don't it?" She didn't answer, so I got a little more aggressive with my strokes and the hair pulling. "I fuck you better than yo' nigga, don't it?" She still didn't say shit. I let go of her completely and pulled out slowly. I caught her off guard when I slid my dick in her ass.

"Oww!" She sung that shit like a coyote howling at the moon. I laughed, as she brought her hands back like she was about to stop me from busting in her ass crack. I smacked her hand. "Unh-unh, move them hands and relax those muscles."

"It hurt, stop," she cried out in pain. "Please stop."

"Tell this fuck nigga who fuck you better," I growled, while steadily pumping inside her tight booty hole.

"You! You!"

"No." I smacked her ass hard and it echoed like thunder. "My name is Coy, so yell my name."

"Coy! Coy! Coy!"

That shit was music to my ears, but I knew I was killing her, so I pulled it out her ass and put it back in her pussy. I placed my hand around her neck and squeezed her throat.

After a few minutes of pounding, I could feel her walls vibrate, contract and massage my dick. My eyes rolled to the back of my head and I could feel my knees buckle. Seconds later, I was exploding inside of her. Stepping back, my dick fell out and it was glazed with her juices.

"Shit!" I wiped the sweat from my forehead, then pulled my pants back up. "Stay right there, don't move." I was winded so I was trying to get my breathing back on track.

"Boy, that thang was fie!" I pulled my gun out my pocket. "But, I'm sorry you gotta tell her goodbye." I placed the gun beside her head and pulled the trigger.

Boca!

Josh was on the floor rolling back and forth crying like a girl. "No! No!" he screamed. I walked over and stood over him, taking aim.

"And for the record, I been hittin' ya baby mama. So, tonight wasn't the first time and I play with ya' kids. Joshana, Jojo, Janiyah and Jayla." His eyes stretched wide when I called them by name.

Boca! Boca!

"That's for my uncle." His body jerked and blood soaked through his shirt. "Now ya' ass dead as a doorknob." I kicked him one last time and put my gun away.

"Good, it took long enough," a voice said from behind. "His ass is worth more to me dead than he is alive."

When I turned around, Crystal was rubbing her ears and walking in my direction. "You shot that shit too close to my head, fool."

"But, did I shoot you though?" She did her infamous eye roll, instead of answering the question. "Good, I didn't think so."

"The duffle bag is in the closet. It's two hundred grand in there." Crystal walked up to me and grabbed my dick. "I'm sucking that dick good tonight. You know that gangster shit turns me on in the worst way."

She tried to kiss me, but I moved my head to the side. Shit wasn't gravy at that moment. "What the fuck he was saying to you in Creole?"

"To get you comfortable, take your gun and kill you." She kneeled down beside his body and closed his eyes.

"What you meant by he's worth more to you dead than alive?"

"He took out an insurance policy for the kids in case something happened to him." Crystal stood up and pulled down her dress. "Hurry up so we can get out of here. We getting a room tonight?"

"Nah. I'm going home tonight." It was time for me to go and check on my babies. It was bad enough that I didn't go home in the first place and to top it all off, I took her phone, so she couldn't call if something was wrong. I knew she wasn't happy, but I didn't care. Her time was up.

***

That night, I crept into the house, just to see what she was doing. I could hear music coming from the bedroom, so it was easy to sneak up on her. When I peeked inside she was standing in the middle of the floor naked, with her back to the door, rubbing lotion all over her body and singing. She had to have just gotten out the shower. I stood there with the duffle bag in my hand, watching her movements.

I'm not like him girl, I'll never lie
Or make you cry
I'll ease the pain, the feelings down inside
Girl it's about time to let him know
You have a real man so he's got to go
Don't just have me in the background
Stop keeping him around
It's about time for him to leave
With open arms you I will receive
It's about time to let him know
That it's about time to let him go

Standing there and seeing her feel the lyrics to the song had me feeling like shit. She made it worse when she turned in my direction. Leilani's face was black and blue from where I punched her in the nose. I watched closely as she applied cocoa butter to her thighs and that's when I noticed they were covered in bruises.

"Damn! What the fuck did I do?" I whispered, unaware that I had caused so much damage to her body.

I could hear her voice over the music. "Time for him to leave you. My open arms will receive you. Time to let him go, time to let him go. Woo."

Leilani broke down and held on to that last note for dear life, like she wanted the Lord to hear her cries. On bended knees, she sang her heart out and her arms followed along with the beat. Her fists were balled up and her eyes were closed, so I knew she was feeling it.

I wanted to go in, but I was afraid of what she was going to say to me. From the looks of things, it seemed as if she was ready to leave me for good. I knew she was tired of my shit, but she didn't understand my issues and the way I was brought up. I would die if she left me. Well, I wouldn't, but somebody would. Leilani belonged to me and she needed to understand that. The piercing sound of her scream snapped me out of my thoughts.

"Why Coy? Why?" She cried. "How could you do these things to me when all I want in this world is you?" Her face was glistening from the tears.

My heart couldn't handle it anymore, so I had to walk in and comfort the love of my life. The woman I wanted to spend the rest of my life with. The moment I stepped inside the room, she jumped when she laid eyes on me.

"I'm sorry, baby. I didn't mean to scare you." She still had her hand over her chest. My approach was gentle, but she still had that frightened look in her teary eyes. Her shoulders even tensed up. *Damn!* I really fucked this girl up. The last thing I ever wanted was for her to be afraid of my presence.

Dropping the duffle bag at my feet, I stepped towards her slowly, but she took a step back. "Coy, please don't hit me again.

I'm begging you." The sound of her voice was soft and gentle and that made me feel like a monster.

"I'm not going to hit you. I just want to hold you." Leilani nodded her head with caution, but she never took her eyes off me. My height and weight intimidated her, so I knew we couldn't have a heartfelt conversation with me looking down at her. I got down on my knees and put my arms around her waist to show her I wasn't a threat. The scent of her sweet-smelling body wash was intoxicating, as I sniffed her skin.

"Baby, I'm sorry about the other day and I mean it. I don't know what comes over me at times. I love you to death and the thought of losing you scares me."

I gently placed my head on her stomach and tightened my grip. My heart fluttered when I felt the baby move. "I can't live without you. Please don't leave me."

My eyes watered up as I begged for her forgiveness. "I promise, I won't hit you again. Please forgive me." This was the first time I cried for a woman, other than my mother and meant it.

Leilani stroked the top of my head gently. "You can't keep doing this to me," she whispered. "I love you, but if I have to leave you, I will."

"You just don't understand." I sobbed.

"Help me, 'cause I don't understand how you can abuse the one you love."

I knew she wanted an explanation and I owed her that much. "When I was younger, I used to witness my alcoholic mammie get beat on the regular. I was small, so there wasn't shit I could do to defend her, even if I wanted to. Most of the fighting happened when I was in bed, but a lot of it happened in my face whenever they got drunk. She wore so many ass whoopings and black eyes that I thought it was natural. Then one day, I asked her why does she put up with it? Do you know what she said?" I looked up to catch her facial expression.

"What?"

I dropped my head. "She said having him in the house was better than getting up to go to work every day, and she had to take the good and the bad. Then she went on to say she just had to work on not getting slick and listening to him more and once I got older, I would go through that with my girlfriend."

"Baby, I'm sorry you had to go through that, but that's not true." She sniffled. "My daddy took care of home and he never put his hands on my mama."

Leilani grabbed my hands from her waist and tugged on them. "Stand up." The bruises on her face were hard to look at, so I turned away.

"You can't look at me?" she whispered, so I shook my head no. "Why not? You did this. So you have to look at it. This is what you wanted me to look like, right? To make me look less attractive."

I couldn't muster up a single word in my defense, so I stared at the window. A few seconds later, she released one of my hands and her fingertips gripped my chin, turning my head in her direction. I blinked a few times, hoping the image would go away, but it didn't. The fresh bruises were still there.

"Just look at me."

We stood face-to-face, looking in one another's eyes. This was a hard task for me and I would rather have my eyes gouged out. My heart ached terribly staring at the aftermath of my vicious wrath. "I didn't mean to do that."

Leilani pointed at the knot on her head. "This is from when you smashed my head against the window." She brought her finger down to her nose. "I think you broke it when you punched me. You don't have to beat me to get your point across. I'm not a puppy in training. It's called communication. All I want is to be treated right by the man I sleep with every night."

We both stood there with tears streaming down our faces, but we were crying for different reasons. I pulled her close to me and hugged her tightly. "Baby, I don't know how to love you without hurting you. Please help me," I begged. "I'll do whatever it takes, just be patient with me and promise you won't leave me."

Leilani squeezed me tight and sighed heavily into my chest. "I promise."

Later on that night I took the first step towards making things right in our relationship. First, I started off by giving back her cellphone and car keys that I confiscated the day before. Then, I gave Leilani twenty thousand dollars out of the money I took from Josh and told her to go shopping.

Chapter 13

Three weeks later

Leilani

Today was going to be a great day for me. My best friend was here for the winter break and I couldn't wait to link up with her. I knew she had so much to tell me about the wonderful college life I was missing out on. The timer on my phone went off, alerting me that it was time to remove the cleanser from my face. Leaning down in the sink, I turned the water on and let it run until it was warm.

When the water was ready, I bent down in the sink and rinsed my face thoroughly. My back was killing me, so I had to hurry up and straighten my back.

At my doctor's visit a few days ago, the doctor told me and Coy the baby weighed six pounds. That's big, considering the fact that I was thirty-two weeks. We still had a long eight weeks to go. By the time I gave birth, the baby would be well over ten pounds and that was scary. I didn't know anything about bringing another human into the world and being fully responsible for them. I finally turned the water off and reached for my towel, but I didn't feel it.

I sucked my teeth. "Don't tell me I left it."

"You looking for this?" Coy asked. Then, I felt him place a small towel in my hand.

"Yes. Thank you, baby." Now I could lift my big ass up.

"You welcome," he replied.

When I dried my face and opened my eyes, Coy was standing behind me. He wrapped his arms around my waist and rubbed my stomach. "I can't wait to meet our son." He smiled sweetly and kissed me on my neck.

I smiled back at him. "Me either." This was the man I fell in love with. I don't know where he got that villain from, but I needed him to keep that part of him away from me.

It had been a while since he put his hands on me and I must say, I was happier than I had been in months. We were spending more time together and I was finally the number-one priority in his life. As far as my happiness was concerned, he did whatever I requested, including taking maternity pictures with me.

"So, where are you and big mouth going?" He smirked.

I had to laugh first, then I smacked him playfully on the arm. "That's not my best friend name."

"Okay, fine. I'll ask you again." He cleared his throat. "So, where are you and Caussia going?"

"That's better. So we're going to lunch and probably the mall afterwards."

"Which mall? Sawgrass?" He tilted his head to the side, awaiting my reply.

"I'm not sure, but that would be a good idea. Maybe I can walk this baby out, so I can have my body back and my internal organs can have their space back." Coy rubbed against me and I could feel his hard dick poking me.

"Yeah, try that, so I can get your insides back too." He cracked up off his own joke and I soon followed. His laughter was so contagious, I couldn't help myself.

"Is that right?"

"Hell, yeah. I'm ready to break you off proper. You too big now and you can only do so much. I like rough sex, pound game and awkward positions." Coy licked my ear and the side of my neck. "You can't take all this right now." He barked like a dog in my ear, while rubbing his dick against my booty.

"Move, silly. I have to finish getting ready." I tried to step away, but he wouldn't let me go. "You gone hold me hostage, huh?"

"Let me get a quickie first," he whispered in my ear.

"I can't, baby, Caussia waiting on me."

"Please, baby. I'll be quick, I promise." He licked my neck, knowing damn well that was my spot. I had to press my thighs together to kill the tingling sensation between my legs, but that was hard to do when he was sucking the hell out of my neck.

"When. I. Come. Back. I. Promise," I was panting so hard I couldn't get my damn words out.

"I can't wait that long. It's too hard you feel it." Coy's hands traveled below my navel until he reached the hood of my vagina. Using his fingers, he spread my petals apart and massaged my clit. My body quivered at his touch and now I was obligated to fulfill his needs, the same way he fulfilled mine.

"Mm," I moaned, biting down on my lip, throwing my head back so he can keep his lips on my neck.

Loosening the front of the towel, I let it fall freely off my upper body. Coy dipped his fingers in and out of my box at a snail's pace. "Ssssss. This. Is. Not. A. Quickie."

"I had to get it wet first." There was some movement behind me, but I was oblivious to what he was doing until he eased his fingers from my center. "Put your hands on the sink." He grabbed the towel and tossed it on the floor.

His hand was on the small of my back, while he rubbed his dick against my opening. After a few strokes, he plunged deep inside and pulled back slowly. He repeated that move several times and I was starting to think he was teasing.

"Fuck me hard," I whispered, surprising myself with such a painful demand.

"You sure 'bout that?"

After putting things into perspective, I realized if I wanted to keep him happy, I would need to engage in the things he wanted to do. So, I sucked it up and prepared myself for some excruciating pain. I rather do it, instead of him cheating on me with his ex. Shit, this might send me into premature labor, but I didn't care, because I was tired of being shaped like a fat-ass elephant. I clenched my eyes together and took a deep breath.

"Yes."

***

"You okay, Leilani?" Caussia asked, as I took baby steps to the car. We had just finished having lunch at BJ's Brew House in Coral Springs.

"Yeah, I'm full." I laughed.

"Oh, okay. I'm just asking, because you moving slow like a sloth." She unlocked the car doors and waited on me to get in first, but of course, I took my time easing down in the front seat.

"I'm big as hell, that's what's wrong. My body is not used to weight." That was only part of the truth, not the entire truth. Something told me to decline his sexual advances before going out, but no, I just had to agree. Then on top of that, my big, bad, bold ass had the nerve to ask for the deluxe package and now I was in pain. I swear, it felt like my bottom was about to fall out.

"We still sliding up on Dontae, or do I need to take you home?" Caussia started the car then pulled out the parking lot.

"We can stop by there for a little bit before I go in." I put on my seatbelt and leaned back in the seat, so I could rest my eyes for a little bit.

"I know you not going to sleep on me?" Caussia was loud like we were in different cars.

"I'm not sleep. I'm resting my eyes until we get there." I really wasn't sleep. "Okay, so tell me about college, since I'm missing out on everything."

"Girl, college is so much fun. I wish you was there with me. It sucks not having my best friend there, but I did meet some cool ass females and they asses love to party. I done been to so many, it don't make sense."

"It's some cute boys out there?" I turned my head in her direction.

"Hell yeah, it is. I met this dude name Dillan and he is hella fine."

"Dillan sounds white." I scrunched my face up.

"Why you looking like that?"

"Girl, you ain't never date no white boy before." The baby started hitting somersaults out the blue. I rubbed my stomach to calm him down. "Woo!" I sighed.

"What's wrong?" Caussia took her eyes off the road to make sure I was good.

"Yeah." I frowned. "He just kicking like crazy, like he on a jungle gym."

"Ooh, I wanna feel it," she shouted in excitement and reached over to touch my stomach. "It feels so weird."

"That's how I was the first time I felt him move." My eyes lit up with so much joy, watching him move around. "I can't wait to meet him."

Caussia moved her hand so she could pay attention to the road. "You not scared."

"A little bit, but Coy said I had nothing to worry about, because he would be right there with me."

She rolled her eyes. "Chi, please. Like he know anything about a baby."

"Well, I guess we gone learn together."

"So, how is the married life going?"

"Girl, we are not married, so cut it out."

"Shit, y'all might as well get married. Y'all shacking up and got a baby on the way. Yeah, that's definitely married life, girl." Caussia tried to give me a high five, but I left her hanging. "Whaattt?" she screeched. "You don't agree?"

"No, 'cause you being funny." Now she had me rolling my eyes and taking deep breaths. "Anyway, things are great between us. He gave me twenty thousand dollars and for Christmas, he bought me a matching necklace and bracelet set, shoes and clothes. He likes spoiling me."

It wouldn't be right if I didn't boast about it and make my life seem like a fairytale. True enough, we were best friends, but right now she was living the life that I desperately wanted. Choosing Coy over my father was the biggest mistake of my life. Not only was I wrong for doing it. I was stupid and he made me pay for it dearly on a daily basis.

"Damn, Leilani, he doing it like that?" Her mouth gaped in surprise.

"Yep."

"Well at least you don't have to feel too bad about your daddy cutting you off, since Coy taking good care of you."

Silence took over the conversation, so I just sat there and fidgeted with my fingers. That was a sensitive subject and I didn't want to dwell on it. I wasn't in the mood to start crying. A small part of me wanted to confide in my best friend because I knew there wouldn't be any judgement on her part. But, the embarrassment wouldn't let me be truthful to her. Over the past five months, I had become good at pretending to be happy. Denial had become my best friend. It was my security blanket to keep me from dealing with reality.

"He at the office by the nail shop across the street from the Lauderhill Mall?"

"Yeah."

Five minutes later, we pulled up to the Navy Recruitment Office where Dontae worked. "I'll go in and get him."

"Okay, I'll be right here."

I opened up the car door and got out. When I walked inside, he was the first face I saw. He had this big ass Kool-Aid smile on his face.

"I'm coming out right now." He stood up and shook the boy's hand he was sitting with.

The building was cold as hell, so I went outside to catch the natural breeze. A December day in Florida could feel like the summer, but today we were fortunate to have a temperature of seventy degrees. That was a blessing within itself. Caussia got out the car and joined me on the sidewalk.

"He coming out?"

"Yeah."

The door opened and Donate walked out and gave me a hug. That smile was still there. "Hey. I'm surprised to see you here."

I laughed and playfully hit him in the arm. "I told you I was coming."

"Yeah, I know, but we haven't talked since you hung up on me when your boyfriend came home. So, I didn't know what to expect. That's why I haven't called you. I'm not trying to get nothing else started with him."

"Well, what the hell happened that I don't know about?" Caussia asked.

"My bad, Caussia. How you doing?" he asked.

"I'm good, but I'm trying to find out what y'all got going on." She put her hands on her hips and waited for an answer. "Cause, I'm lost."

Detective Caussia was officially on the case and this was the exact thing I was trying to avoid. *Damn!* Why he had to say something? Now she wasn't gone let it rest.

"It's nothing, Caussia. Just a misunderstanding." My eyes drifted off into another direction. I was trying my best to hold it together. No one would ever understand my mental state and I wasn't trying to force it either.

"Well shit, help me get out of the state of confusion." When I didn't respond, she asked Dontae. "You might as well tell, since she won't."

"I said too much already. She'll tell you when she ready." Dontae grabbed my arm gently. "Can I talk to you for a second, please?"

Instead of responding, I allowed him to whisk me away so we could talk in private. "I want to apologize for what just happened. I assumed she knew, since y'all are best friends."

"Apology accepted." My sudden mood change made it difficult to hide the dry remark.

"You sure about that cause it doesn't sound like it."

Dontae did absolutely nothing to me and here I was, ready to jump down his throat about nothing. The only way out was to force a smile and pretend like everything was good at home.

"It's okay, really. Besides, you didn't do anything wrong back there. This pregnancy just has me so emotional and depressed all the time and that makes it hard to cope."

"Whew! I'm relieved now. The last thing I wanted was for you to be upset with me." Dontae grabbed my hand and looked into my eyes. "We had a good friendship and now that I'm back,

I want it to stay that way. There's no need to feel that way, because I'm just a phone call away. All you have to do is utilize the number."

Chemistry was definitely in the air. The way his thumb stroked the palm of my hand signaled there was a possibility he wanted more. "I agree." That was all I could say in response to all he said.

"Okay, well give me a hug and let's get back over there, before Caussia comes over."

Dontae pulled me close to him and hugged me tight. "I want some alone time with you. I've missed you and we have some catching up to do."

It was that moment that I wondered what my life would be like if we would've worked through our differences and stayed together. He was definitely living his best life and I could've been right beside him, traveling the world during my school breaks. After Dontae let go of me, I spotted Caussia walking in our direction, with her hand resting on her hip.

"I knew it wouldn't be long before you walked over Ann Bishop."

Thanks to Dontae, I was feeling a lot better and I was definitely going to take him up on his offer. There was no telling when Coy would resort back to his old ways and I needed to be prepared for the day he snapped.

Chapter 14

Coy

"Why you picking out girl clothes?" Leilani asked, while rummaging through the clothing rack at Children's Place.

"I'm getting them for my niece, is that okay with you?" I picked up one last outfit and tossed it into the shopping bag.

"I'm just asking, because I was a little confused." Leilani tossed the clothes in her bag with an attitude and gave me a certified death stare like she wanted to slap the black off my face. "I'm ready to go."

That girl kept an attitude, but I figured it was because she was just hormonal and shit. It wasn't my fault she was tired of being pregnant. Shit, I was tired too. Tired of her whining, crying, that fucked-up attitude and her inability to take the dick. I was doing my best at keeping my hands to myself for the sake of my son, but that was like pulling teeth. Several times in the mall, I was tempted to go upside her head and catch a case. A few more months and I was gone kick her ass for the old and new.

Leilani rudely dropped her bag on the counter in front of the cashier, while mumbling under her breath. The girl looked at her and then at me, before grabbing the bag and forcing a phony smile.

"Did you find everything okay?" Her customer service was better than mine, because I wouldn't have said shit to her nasty ass.

"Of course I did, since there was no one here to assist me." Leilani snidely replied with her nose tooted in the air like the girl had bad breath or some shit. The expression on the cashier's face proved she wanted to say something back to her, but she needed her job more than she needed a clap back.

"Oh, well I wasn't aware that you needed any assistance."

"I apologize for her rudeness. You didn't do anything wrong." I stepped up and moved Leilani to the side. It ain't like she was paying for shit anyway. "She's having a bad day."

"Yeah and I wonder why." Her brown slits cut me deep when she rolled her eyes.

I placed all of my items on the counter along with her stuff and gave her the side eye. What she didn't want to do in public, let alone in private, was go toe to toe with me.

"Don't reach, Lani. Please don't. That's not what you wanna do." Leilani turned on her heels and stormed out the store. So, I turned my attention back to the cute female with the natural, curly hair. Her skin was honey dipped, just like her hair and I definitely wanted to taste that.

"You must've really pissed her off." She smirked a little.

"Yeah, but she'll be alright." I leaned against the counter and licked my lips seductively, while staring at her breasts. They were puffed up in a nice fitted bra and button-up shirt that she left slightly open. "So, where yo' man at?"

Honey blonde looked at me and smiled. "I don't have one."

"You sure about that?"

"I don't have a reason to lie." After she was done scanning the items she placed them in several bags and sat it on the counter. "Your total is two twenty-seven, forty-four."

I reached down inside my pocket and pulled out my cash flow that was neatly folded and held by a rubber band. Her eyes didn't leave my hands until I handed her three, crispy blue-face hunnids. She placed the money in the register and counted out my change.

"Here you go."

"Nah, you keep that and take this too." I handed her my business card. "There's a lot more where that came from, if you call me."

"My name is Whitney." She grabbed the card from my hand and slid it slowly inside her bra. Not once did she take her eyes off me. Our attraction was mutual, and I could see the seduction in her eyes.

"Nice to meet you, Whitney, I'm Coy."

"The feeling is mutual, Coy." The way my name rolled off her tongue made me picture something else rolling down it. The piercing in her mouth made my dick press hard against my zipper. My mind was in the gutter with thoughts of her pretty little red pussy lips holding onto my dick, while I knock the screws loose.

Two females walked in the store talking loud and laughing even louder, interrupting my wild thoughts. Whitney glanced at them briefly, then back at me. "You better get going before your baby mama come back in here."

"Yeah, you right."

"I'll call you later on when I get off." She hesitated. "If it's not too late."

"Bet that up, boo. I'll be waiting."

***

Leilani sat with her arms folded during the ride home, peering out the window. She hadn't said a word to me since we left Children's Place. The music wasn't loud, but I turned it down further. "Bae, what you want to eat?"

Leilani sat there like I wasn't talking to her.

"Bae, you hungry?"

Still nothing.

"Leilani!" I shouted. She was really pissing me off. "Yo' ass hear me talking to you."

"Don't ask me shit. Just take me home and worry about the bitch at the register."

A nigga was stone cold busted. She had to be watching me from the outside. I played dumb anyway. "What the fuck you talm 'bout?"

Leilani turned in her seat and stared at me with piercing, cold eyes. "You think I'm so fuckin' stupid. I know you got that bitch number when I walked out the store."

"No I didn't. Now why in the fuck would I be hollerin' at another bitch when I'm with you? That's just dumb."

"Because you dumb and I'm not your bitch either," she huffed.

"Lani, chill out, 'cause I wasn't calling you a bitch." I ignored the fact that she called me dumb, because I was busted and I couldn't deny that. But, I wasn't about to confess to shit she couldn't prove.

"Fuck you, Coy. I'm sick of going through bullshit with you." When those last words left her mouth, I reached over and popped her right in it.

She grabbed her mouth and screamed. "Go ahead, beat me all you want to and kill me while you at it. I would rather be dead than to constantly go through hell with you on a daily basis."

Honestly, that shit hurt a nigga heart to hear her say she would rather be dead. Damn, I guess I was really fucked up. I grabbed her hand and pulled it to my mouth so I could kiss it. "Lani, I'm sorry for hitting you, but I swear, I ain't holla at that chick and I didn't call you a bitch either. You my queen and the mother of my son. I love you and I wouldn't disrespect you like that."

Leilani didn't look at me or acknowledge anything I said. True enough, I was lying about my actions, but my feelings were real for her. The bitch in the mall was just somebody I wanted to fuck. Nothing more, nothing less. I was where I wanted to be.

"Coy, I fuckin' saw you hand her something and it wasn't money." She snatched her hand away and hit me with that evil ass stare again. "Just stop. You always lying and hurting me. One day I won't be here and that will be the day you miss what you had."

"And you think I'm gone let you leave me? Yeah, a'ight. You must be crazy or them prenatal vitamins polluting your fuckin' brain. I'm never letting you go."

I placed my hand on her belly and rubbed it in a circular motion to remind her that we were invested into one another. "You and me in this forever, baby, so you might as well get that out your head right now."

"You need to do better or I will leave you and that's my promise to you."

Clearly, she ain't heard a word I said. The light had just turned yellow, so that was my chance to get my point across. Slowly smashing down on the brake, I came to a complete stop and moved my hand from her belly and grabbed her face gently.

"Leilani, I love you." I leaned over and planted a sensual kiss to her warm cheek. "I'll kill you before I let you go and that's my promise to you."

Lani closed her eyes and for a second, I could've sworn she stopped breathing for a split second, while I rubbed my face against hers. No matter how she felt at that moment, that wouldn't change the way I was feeling. It didn't matter if I cheated or not, she better not try and leave me. I would hate to make good on my promise, because idle threats were not something I was involved in. Whatever I said, I meant, and I followed through with it.

***

Before I took Leilani home, I stopped by the Dutch Pot to get her something to eat, since I didn't know how long I would be gone. When I pulled up in front of the building, Leilani was mumbling under her breath. Majority of the shit she was saying I couldn't understand, but one thing was clear. She wasn't happy about me leaving her right at that moment. I knew she wanted me to come upstairs, but I had an errand to run.

"Always going somewhere, but want me to stay in the house. I must be the biggest fuckin' idiot in the planet." She continued to mumble, while snatching up her food and the bags of clothing we got for the baby.

"I heard that."

"Good," she snapped.

"You can't carry all that, just go upstairs, and I'll bring it up when I get back."

"Fine." Leilani slung the bags in my lap and slammed the car door.

"This bitch gone send me to prison. I swear." I put the clothes in the passenger seat and put the car in drive before I pulled off. "A nigga really trying to be calm, but she is pushing it."

Before I could make it down the street, my phone rang. I picked it up and hit the green icon. "Yeah."

"Where you at?" Crystal spoke calmly.

"On my way to your house. Why?" I hooked a right onto Oakland Park.

"Oh, I was just making sure you didn't forget about us."

Whenever she wanted something, she knew how to calm her ass down. Now what she wanted was the question. "Nah, I didn't forget. I'll be there in a few minutes." Silence lingered for a while. "Is that all you wanted?"

"Can you stop by Pizza Hut for me? I ordered food for the kids, but they backed up and don't know how long it's gone take."

"Yeah. I'll get it."

"Thanks."

"No problem."

Pizza Hut was on smash when I got there. It was like everyone and they mammy wanted pizza. The wait wasn't long at all since they had her order ready, so I was able to do an in and out with no problem.

When I pulled up at Crystal's house, the Range Rover parked on the side of the house caught my attention. It looked familiar and that immediately made my forehead wrinkle. Today had to be "try Coy" day or some shit, because she had me fucked up too. Both of my hoes were testing my patience. The pizza box was hot in my hands, but I ignored the heat that blended perfectly to the heat spewing from my body. The door swung open and Crystal stood there in a pair of tights that were wedged inside her fat pussy, exposing her camel toe. The tank top she was wearing revealed her erect, chocolate chip nipples. She thought she was slick, trying to knock me off my game. That wasn't happening though. She had me fucked up on every aspect of the word.

"What the fuck this nigga truck doing here?" I shoved the pizza boxes in her hand.

"What the fuck, man? This shit hot." She adjusted the boxes in her hand. "His mama gave it to me, why?"

"What the fuck for?"

"I do have his kids, idiot."

"Well, don't ask me to pay the note, because I'm not doing it." I turned around to go back to the car.

"The truck is paid for, so I don't have to pay for nothing. And even if I did, you would've paid for it if I asked you to."

My first thought was that the nigga died for nothing. He paid cash for a Range Rover and had the audacity to not pay my uncle his bread. Oh well, he made his bed and now he was resting in it eternally. I grabbed the bags from the car and went inside the house.

"Coy!" the girls shouted and ran in my direction. I dropped the bags on the sofa, knelt and gave them all hugs.

"Wassup, cuties? Did y'all miss me?"

"Yeah," they all shouted.

"I missed y'all too. Go get some pizza and save me a slice, okay?"

"Okay," Jojo replied.

Jayla was the baby and she was standing up in her playpen, positioned in front of the television. *Mickey Mouse Club* was the only show that kept her quiet, but Jayla became excited when she saw me. She bounced up and down until I was standing in front her.

"Da-Da."

I leaned down into the mini prison that was holding her hostage and took her into my arms. "Hey fat mama. Did you miss daddy?"

She smiled and hit me with that baby talk.

Jayla was my daughter, but we kept it low-key to keep Josh out of our business. The plan to extort money from him came from my uncle Duke, but I made it my business to get Crystal involved. At one point in time, she did love him, but he cheated on her and had an outside baby. After that, she developed a strong hate for him and then we started fucking around. While I was plotting and preying on her weakness, I ended up getting her pregnant.

No one knew I was the father, nor did they suspect it, but all of that was about to change sooner or later. With Josh out the picture, I no longer had to worry about the safety of my daughter while she was around him. The idea alone made me sick, but it had to be done and now it was over. I knew once Leilani found out about Jayla, she was going to be hurt. But, that happened before her time so technically she had no reason to be upset. I would just tell her I recently found out, although, I knew it from the beginning. That was the issue between Crystal and I, she wanted me to tell Leilani, but I wasn't ready to come clean about my secret just yet.

As I bounced Jayla in my arms, I walked towards the sofa where I dropped the bags. "Daddy missed you so much and I bought you some clothes."

We sat down on the couch, while Crystal fed the girls. When she was done, she walked over and stood in front of me. "Is she the only one you bought stuff for?"

"Do I ever come here and not bring them something?" I kept my cool for the sake of the kids. My phone vibrated inside my pocket, so I pulled it out and tossed it beside me. Whoever it was could wait, because I was spending time with my baby.

"No." Crystal crossed her arms. "I was just curious, that's all. Because if you didn't, I was gone tell you to take it in the room, so they couldn't see. You know how they get."

"Yeah, I know and that's why I bought them something as well," I replied, while showing Jayla her clothes and giving her the stuffed animal, I picked up as well.

Although Crystal's other daughters belonged to Josh, I never treated them differently, despite my feelings for him. They had nothing to do with what was going on, so I left them out of it and treated them as if they were my own kids. After all, they were innocent.

"Thanks. I appreciate that." She leaned down and kissed me. "I'll show you just how much I do later."

"Not while the kids up. You know how I feel about that."

"They will be in the room watching a movie." She sat down beside me.

"Can you go on the other couch, please? You are interfering with daddy-daughter time," I said in a joking manner. Sex was the furthest thing from my mind.

"That's fine. I don't have to sit by y'all." Crystal stood up and sat on the sofa adjacent to where I was sitting.

"Mommy, can I get some more pizza?" Joshana, the eldest daughter asked.

"Go ahead."

"Mommy, me too?" Jojo shouted.

"Shana, give your sister another slice." Crystal pulled her feet beneath her and turned the station.

"Okay, Mommy."

Crystal was ratchet as they came, but I couldn't take away the fact that she was a damn good mother to her kids. They always had their hair done, nice clothes and she spent time with them on a regular basis. I never had to question my daughter's well-being. She never put me before her kids and that was before she had my baby. When she looked at me with admiration it almost made me feel bad, for not trying to make it work for the sake of our child. I knew she loved me, but I couldn't be what or who she wanted me to be. I loved her because she gave me my first child, but I wasn't in love with her. Our relationship was too toxic and the only thing I saw coming from that was a murder case.

"Coy?" she whispered. Her eyes were low and her facial expression told me a serious question was about to follow. I was almost certain I knew what she was about to speak on. So, bring on the bullshit.

Chapter 15

Crystal

By the look on Coy's face, he had to know what I was talking about. I knew because I saw this look one too many times.

"What's up?" he asked.

I always fumbled with my fingers and bit my lip whenever I was nervous. "Have you told Leilani about Jayla?"

His silence made him appear to be guilty, before I spoke a word. Instead of saying something, he shook his head no.

"What are you waiting on?" I looked over at the kids to make sure they weren't paying us any attention. "I've been silent about this long enough and I'm not doing it anymore. Jayla will be one soon and I've dealt with this alone long enough. It's not fair to me or her."

"Crystal, you're right, but it's complicated right now and I need more time. I'm not ready to break her heart just yet."

"Break her heart?" I repeated, while rocking in my seat. "What the fuck do you mean you not ready to break her heart just yet? Nigga, you been did that."

Coy just sat there with a stupid look on his face. "Hmm. I get it now. You don't want to say anything because she pregnant? So, it's fuck me and Jayla?"

"You know it's not like that. I love my daughter and I take care of her. Anything she needs, I get it for her and you know that."

"Wow!" I nodded my head up and down with my face balled up. "So, it's fuck me, then?"

"Crystal, just stop."

Following his eyes, I turned towards my girls at the kitchen table. They were tuned in. "Girls, go in the room please. Joshana make sure they wash their hands."

"Come on, little babies." Joshana stood up and waited on them to follow her lead.

"I'm not a baby," Jojo pouted. "I'm a big girl."

"You are a baby girl and so is Janiyah." Joshana grabbed Janiyah's hand and ushered them down the hallway.

When it was safe to talk, I looked into Coy's deceitful ass lies. "How could you do this to me?" The water in my eyes started to build and I could feel myself on the verge of breaking down.

"Come on, Crystal. Don't do this to me. You know we can't be together. We're too toxic."

"I know what that means."

"And what is that?"

"You want someone you can control. Someone who won't fight you back. I know you better than you know yourself. I love you, but I guess that doesn't mean shit to you, huh?"

"You know I love you for giving me my first child. That will never change." He kissed Jayla on the top of her head.

"She's the only reason, I see." I had to sit up in my seat off of that one. "I set my kids father up for you. I allowed you to take him away from them, under the false pretense we would be together and you lied to me."

Coy hurt me deeply and he didn't give a single fuck, but that was my fault. He had me feeling stupid. It was all good though, because I wasn't about to be the only one hurting. As I stood up slowly, I stopped in front of him and took Jayla from his arms.

"What you doing?"

"It's time for you to leave. I'm done with this and you. Congratulations, on the baby."

"Damn, it's like that?" Coy stood up, scratching his head in confusion.

"You made it this way. Now please leave."

"A'ight."

Coy walked past me, down the hallway, avoiding all eye contact. I thought he was going to tell the girls bye, but then I heard the bathroom door close. When I looked at the sofa, I realized he left his phone. My envious ways got the best of me, so I picked up his phone and scrolled through his call log, until I found the number I was looking for and stored it in my memory bank. To make sure I didn't forget it, I grabbed my phone from the counter and locked the number in. I also noticed that he had a text message from another female that said, *"Hey it's me, Whitney. The one you met at the mall. I get off at 9pm and I would love to see you afterwards."*

"And he still cheating with his nasty ass."

As I looked down the hallway, the door opened and he walked out. He had a unit on his face, but I didn't care. I was tired of playing games with him and it was obvious he wasn't trying to do anything about it. Coy stopped in front of me and kissed Jayla once more, but he kept his lips on her cheek for a long period of time with his eyes closed.

"I love you so much, mama." He made no attempt to acknowledge anything I said previously. Instead, he snatched his keys up and slammed the door on his way out. I waited until he pulled off to call the number.

"Hello."

"Is this Leilani?"

"Who is this?" she snapped.

"Crystal."

"Why the fuck you calling me? And, how did you get my number?"

"Listen, I'm not calling you on no bullshit. I'm calling because I have some things to tell you about Coy I think you need to know."

"And why should I listen to anything out your mouth?"

"Because I have information you want to know. I don't have anything to gain at this point and I'm done dealing with him for good this time."

"Well, I don't believe you." Leilani had a real attitude, but I couldn't blame her. If another woman was coming to me as such, she would have to catch a fade.

"You'll believe me when I show you the proof. So, can you meet me at the park on Oakland, across the street from the library?"

"Why should I trust this is not a set-up for you to try and jump me?"

"You should believe me, because I know that he went to the mall today and bought my daughters some clothes."

Leilani was caught off guard and I could hear her heavy breathing in the phone. "What?"

"He bought them clothes from Children's Place. So, tell me that I'm lying now." I paused for a second. "I'm bringing my kids with me, so come now."

"Okay." She finally agreed and we ended the call.

***

Forty-five minutes had passed and I was still sitting in the park, watching my kids play on the playground. Leilani hadn't showed up and when I called her, she didn't answer. Maybe she had second thoughts and decided not to show up after all. It was all good though because in a few weeks I would be MIA. Josh had a life insurance policy in place for the girls for half a million dollars. I decided to pack my kids up and move to Texas for a fresh start in life. I made so many mistakes and it was time for me to be a better person. My friend moved there last year and she loved it.

The sun was extremely hot and I was sweating my ass off, but my girls didn't care, because they were having a blast. Jayla and I were sitting underneath the pavilion and there wasn't a lick of wind blowing. Florida was just hot and humid for no damn reason.

"Fat ma, you ready to go?" I sat her on the table and played peek-a-boo with her. When I covered my face, she tried to move my hands.

"Boo!" Jayla giggled and her little eyes closed. There was no denying she looked exactly like her dog-ass daddy. They had the same eyes, nose and grade of hair. Her head was full of small afro puffs. I covered my eyes once more.

"Boo!" My baby was really cracking up on the little game we were playing. She was such a happy little girl. The only time she cried was when she was hungry.

The sound of a car horn caught my attention and when I looked up, I saw a BMW. Seeing Leilani carrying Coy's child did something to my spirit and brought on a flashback from when she jumped on me at Coy's apartment. Just thinking about it made me want to fight, but that wasn't why I wanted to meet her. She walked up to where I was sitting.

"Sorry for the wait, but he was too busy trying to keep me in the house for some apparent reason." Leilani looked at Jayla and smiled. "She's cute."

"Thank you."

"So, what do you need to show me?"

"Have a seat. You don't want to be standing when you hear this." The second she sat down, I continued. "This is going to be hard to hear, but it has to be said. If not, Coy will just continue to play games with the both of us—"

Leilani interrupted me. "What do you mean us? Coy and I are together, not y'all."

"That's what he's telling you. Coy and I have been dealing with one another for almost two years now."

"That's not what I saw that day you came to the house. He told you to your face that we were together and he showed you that." She stated with great belief.

"Yeah that's what he said in front of you, but that didn't stop him from coming to my house. That's where he was that day you called because you wanted to go to the hospital. And, when he was missing for those two days he was with me."

Leilani sat there and took in everything I was telling her. However, something told me that she already knew that and nothing I was saying was a surprise.

"I know you probably don't believe me, but it's true."

Her eyes were empty and dark as she replied. "I believe you."

"And it hurts me to tell you this, but this is his daughter Jayla." I turned my baby around so she could get a good look at her. "She looks just like him."

Leilani was in complete shock and her expanded eyes told me so. "What? No. Coy doesn't have kids."

"He lied to you and I'll show you." I pulled out my cellphone and thumbed through the gallery. When I found the pictures I was looking for, I handed her my phone.

"Those are pictures of me and him when I gave birth to her eleven months ago. There's also a video of them together. I don't have a reason to lie to you because after today, Coy will never see me or his daughter again. I'm done with him for good. So, you don't have to worry about me anymore. But, I will say that you should be worried about some female name Whitney, he met at the mall today. When I was looking through his phone, she texted him saying she wanted to meet up with him when she got off work tonight."

Leilani scrolled through my pictures and I could see the tears in her eyes. Her hands trembled slightly, as she watched the video of him singing to Jayla. Being a woman, I felt her pain and ultimately I felt bad for her. My confession crushed her, but I wanted to be honest with her for once. Coy was full of shit and a no good ass dog. She needed to know what to expect from him if she decided to stay. Hopefully, our talk would make her leave while she could.

"I can't believe he would lie to me about this. My life is ruined because of him." She handed me back the phone and wiped her eyes with the back of her hand. "If I would've listened to my daddy, I could've been in college right now."

"Leilani, I'm sorry. I really am, but you need to get out while you can. Coy is preying on your innocence and the love you have for him."

"If you feel that way, why are you still fucking him? And why tell me this now?" she sniffled.

"At the end of the day I'm a woman and I loved Coy, but we can't be together. He told me it was because we're too toxic. But the truth is, he can't control me and when he hits me, I fight back and he don't like that. No offense, but he likes weak women. The ones who won't fight him back."

"I see." She nodded her head, but I could tell she wasn't paying me any attention. Her focus was on Jayla. "She does look like him," Leilani admitted.

The girls were chasing one another and laughing loud and he eyes shifted in their direction. "Are those your kids too?"

Before I could respond, Janiyah ran up to me. "Mommy, is Daddy coming?"

"No, baby. Now go finish playing." She ran off to catch up with her sisters.

"Coy is not their father."

"They're who he bought the clothes for?" she asked.

"Yes. From day one, he always looked out for my girls. He's actually good with the kids, but he's horrible in relationships." I tried to laugh it off and make light of the situation, but Leilani didn't. Her tone and expression was serious.

She held her stomach and sighed with her eyes closed. "I need to go."

"Are you okay?" My question was genuine and I didn't want her going into premature labor.

"I don't feel well."

Leilani turned away from me quickly and dropped her head towards the ground. The sound of fluid hitting the sidewalk made me cringe. On instinct, I stood up and rushed over to where she was sitting. She was doing her best to not throw up on herself, but her stomach was in the way. I held her hair so she didn't throw up on that as well. When she was done, I went back to the stroller and grabbed Jayla's diaper bag to get some wipes.

"Here you go."

She took them from my hand. "Thanks."

"No problem. You should get home now and again, I'm sorry about everything."

After she left, I loaded my kids in the truck and went home. Sooner or later I knew Coy would be calling or either stopping by because of what I did. He had been warned on many occasions that I would tell, but he didn't take me serious. It was cool though, because today was going to make him out to be a believer.

Chapter 16

Leilani

My daddy didn't raise no fool, so when Crystal said she wanted to meet up with me, I was skeptical. I thought of a dozen reasons why I shouldn't go and two dozen reasons why I should. When I finally agreed to go, I made sure I brought my mace and knife just in case it was a setup and I had to give her face a makeover. But as it turned out, her reason was valid, and she was telling the truth about the man that I thought loved me and me only.

On my way home, I listened to Anthony's Hamilton, "Her Heart" and cried like a newborn baby. Coy lied to me and betrayed me in the worst way humanly possible. Not only did he cheat with her, but he was still sleeping with her and had a baby. Granted, it was before my time, but he didn't even have the decency to tell me the truth about his daughter.

When I got to the house he wasn't there, and I was happy that I didn't have to encounter him. Crystal had already gave me the heads up he was meeting up with the girl he met at the mall. And of course, I knew who it was because I confronted him about it and he lied once again. The hurt I was feeling turned into hate very quickly and I wanted nothing else to do with him. My mind was made up and I was leaving him. Time wasn't on my side, so I stuffed my bag with clothes and other necessities I would need expeditiously. Everything else could be replaced. Knowing Coy, he would change the locks and throw my belongings in the trash. His lying, cheating ass was going to be in for a rude awakening whenever he made it home, because I wasn't going to be there. He broke my heart for the last time and there was no coming back from that.

After spending twenty long minutes in the house, I finally made a break for the door. My heart was racing because I was afraid he would catch me before I made it to the promise land.

While walking at a fast pace I constantly prayed that I wouldn't run into him.

The elevator was only a few feet away so I was almost there, but then I realized that was the way he came up to the apartment. Pivoting on my feet, I spent full circle and fled in the direction of the stairwell. Technically, I was a woman on the run and needed my escape to be swift. If he caught me I knew that would be a fight and honestly, I had no more fight in me.

My legs moved at a hundred miles per hour, step by step like the roadrunner. I held onto the rail to keep from falling and injuring myself and my baby. When I got to the bottom and attempted to push the door, it flew open on its own and I tumbled forward. My heart dropped in my ass right away and it felt like I was about to defecate on myself.

"Slow down, l'il mama. You okay?" The gentleman coming through the door grabbed me to keep me from falling.

It was such a relief that it wasn't Coy. If it was, I would've passed out right then and there. No explanation.

"Um. Yeah, I'm fine." I felt dizzy for a moment, so I grabbed my head and shook it from side to side. "Sorry about that."

"Nah, you good. Do you need help?" He finally let me go.

"I'm okay. Thanks." The gentleman stepped to the side and I hightailed it out of the stairwell until I reached my car. Inside, I locked the doors and took a deep breath, then a few quick ones. I just didn't know how the hell my life turned for the worst like that. I've always been a good girl and I knew for a fact I didn't deserve to be treated like shit. Coy was certainly not the man he portrayed to be.

Finally starting the car, I put it in drive and pulled off fast. There was so much going on in my life and I didn't know where to go or who to turn to. Caussia was gone back to school and my nerves weren't strong enough to call Dontae. After I drove on I-95 for a while I got off on my old exit, en route to my old home. My father was the only person who could help me and God knew I needed him more than I've needed him in my life. Hopefully, he wouldn't push me away. Months had passed and forgiveness was in order.

Throughout the remainder of the drive, I practiced my "I'm sorry" speech a dozen times. It didn't matter if I had to beg. All I wanted him to do was hug me, tell me that he loved me and forgave his baby girl for the terrible mistake I made.

When I pulled into the driveway, my palms were very sweaty and my body trembled from fear of rejection. It took a minute for me to get out the car and stand on the very porch, he put me out on. Scared wasn't the word as I knocked on the door and waited for him to answer. One minute had passed when I finally heard the locks on the door become disengaged. My heart rate sped up and when the door opened slowly, I became disappointed when I saw that it was my mother.

"Well, well, look what the hurricane blew this way." She leaned against the door with that same stupid smirk on her face. "Why are you on my porch? Shouldn't you be living happily ever after with your baby daddy?"

My heart was already broken and I felt worthless and low, so I didn't need to be kicked while I was down on my knees prepared to beg my way back in. Diane had to be the worst mother in history and if I had my way, she would've never come back inside that house. Her and my father would've gotten a divorce before she completed rehab.

"Why do you hate me so much? What have I done to you to make you feel this way about me?" The tears built up in my eyes immediately and made their way down my face. "You really hate the fact that me and dad were close?"

Diane laughed with no remorse, as if I said a joke or some shit. If she wasn't my mother I would've slapped the shit out of her. "Hate you? No. Dislike you? Yes."

She stepped closer, poking her head further out the door. "From the time you could walk and talk you have taken the attention from your father that was reserved for me. He always thought you were something special, so he placed you on a pedestal. And what did you do? You turned around and became exactly what I knew you would be. Pregnant out of wedlock and a drop out."

"I remind you of your past, huh?" I shot back. "Well, allow me to fill you in on a little secret. After I have this baby, I will go to college and I will be successful. Mark my words. Now, where is my father? I need to see him."

"He doesn't want to see you, so I advise you to leave my house, because you are not welcome here."

"Diane, who's at the door?" The sound of my father's voice made my heart skip a beat. Suddenly, I smiled on the inside. After all the months that passed us by, I was finally going to see him.

"It's your daughter."

"What?" My father walked up behind my mother and looked me square in the eyes. He was silent and appeared to be taken aback at my presence, but he didn't say a word.

"Daddy, I need to talk to you please. I'm sorry for everything." The sound of my voice was shaky. His expression was blank, and it seemed as if he was contemplating on what he should say. Or, if he should say anything all.

"Umm." He hesitated for a moment and Diane took that as her opportunity to jump in it.

"Don't let her come here and make you second-guess your decision. If you can't find it in your heart to forgive Aniya, then you will not forgive her either."

My father glared down at her and spoke sternly through clenched teeth. "Diane, be quiet. I'm a grown-ass man, I pay the bills and I make the rules. She's still my daughter, so why don't you go inside and let me handle this?"

Diane mumbled something underneath her breath, before stomping off like a child. He stepped down onto the porch and closed the door. It was such a relief to hear he was going to finally talk to me. However, his tone of voice shifted my mood in the opposite direction.

"What is it that you want, Leilani? You've caused enough havoc in my life already, so I hope you didn't come here to make things worse?"

"Daddy, I'm sorry. All my life, you've been proud of me and it hurts me to think you could possibly hate me for the decisions I made."

"Leilani, I don't hate you. I'm disappointed in you for the poor decisions you made. The fact that I gave you space and allowed you to date someone like Coy, was my fault. If I wasn't too busy treating him like the son I never had, none of this shit would've happened."

"I know, but I want to come home. Please." I begged. "I'm not ready for this. It's too much for me. I just want to be your princess again."

When I attempted to reach for his hand, he tried shoving it in his pocket, but I was determined to get my point across through touching.

"That's not possible, baby, and I'm sorry. You are about to be a mother and I told you not to bring a baby home. I'm nobody's grandfather."

Teardrops surfaced in the lids of his eyes, but he turned his head to keep me from seeing them. "You just don't understand how I've sacrificed so much for my family. The risks I took to make sure you were awarded with a good life. I wanted the best for you and threw it all away for some in-house dick."

"Daddy, I do understand, and I need you more than I ever needed you in my life. I don't know who Coy is anymore. He's changed on me completely and I can't do this by myself."

My daddy gently moved his hand away from mine and looked deeply into my shattered soul. "I'm sorry, Leilani, but that's the man you chose and the bed you made. Now you must sleep in it. Coy warned you he was the king of his castle, so you might as well get used to that."

He took a step back and grabbed the door handle. "I have work to do, but it was good seeing you. Good luck with the baby."

And just like that, he walked inside the house and closed the door, leaving me standing on the porch feeling dumber than I did before I came over. The fact was, he didn't love me anymore because if he did, he would've forgave me and held me tightly in his arms. As I walked away with my head held low, the tears were pouring heavy like rain. I got into my car and screamed loud. I was pissed at myself for getting myself involved with a bunch of bullshit. My ass could've been in college living my best life, but no, I thought we were in love and about to live happily ever after. Coy had me fooled in the worst way, but I couldn't lie, I still loved him. No matter how hard I tried to hate him. He was my first in everything and I knew it would be hard to break free from him.

My heart and mind were pulling me in two different places all at once. It felt like I was about to go crazy. My heart was telling me to just go back home, since I had no place to go. That we could work on our issues and once the baby was born things would get better. Meanwhile, my mind was screaming, *run bitch run. The nigga is crazy, and he will never change. You gone stay getting cheated on and getting your ass beat. Leave that nigga alone.* A part of me had a feeling he wasn't going to change and the other part of me wanted to give him a chance. After all, our baby would be entering the world soon, and I did want my child to grow up in a two-parent home. I needed someone to confide in without judgement. Someone I could trust and had my best interest at heart and I knew just who to call. Without further hesitation, I called him up.

"Hello."

"Dontae, are you busy?" I asked, while silently praying he didn't have company or was on a date, because I truly needed a friend right at that moment.

"No. What's going on?"

"I just need someone to talk to and I don't know where to go. My life is a mess and I can't take it anymore."

"Just relax. Stop getting yourself worked up. I'm at Chipotle getting me something to eat. I'll grab you something as well, just meet me at my apartment. I'm about to text you the address."

"Okay."

Chapter 17

Leilani

After sitting in the parking lot of Dontae's apartment complex for close to forty-five minutes, a set of bright lights shined in my eyes, as it parked directly in front of me. Dontae hopped out the car carrying a brown bag and a Kool-Aid smile, so I got out with my bag in my hand and closed the door. His happiness was short lived when he stood face-to-face close to me and witnessed my sadness.

"You've been crying, haven't you?" Dontae shook his head and frowned in disgust. There was no need in replying, because he called me out before I had a chance to start. "I don't know why you put up with that bullshit from that clown-ass nigga."

Dontae grabbed the bag from my hand. "Come on, let's go inside before the food gets cold." I followed behind him like I was a lovestruck, lost puppy.

Dontae lived in a quiet neighborhood in Coral Springs, directly behind the mall. We walked inside the lobby area and waited on the elevator. On the way up, we remained silent. The only sound that could be heard was the dinging noise when the doors opened up on the fifth floor.

"Make a left and go to door 504."

The apartment was down the hall in a dark corner. I stepped to the side so he could unlock the door. When I crossed the threshold, I was amazed at the decor of the apartment. Dontae had OCD, so it wasn't a surprise that nothing was out of place. The living room area was a mixture of dark brown, beige, burgundy and gold. It complemented the dark brown leather sofa and love seat.

"Come in and make yourself comfortable. If you need to use the bathroom, it's down the hall on the right."

"Thanks."

As I walked over to the couch, I scoped out the photos he had posted to see if I could spot a female in any of them. Ever since we reconnected, he never mentioned if he was seeing someone or not. It felt good to plop down on the sofa and take a load off. In his presence I felt safe.

"You can turn on the TV if you like. I'll be right back." Dontae disappeared down the hallway. I looked at my phone and Coy still hadn't called me yet. That was surprising because I figured he would've done so by now, especially since I had the meet up with Crystal. Maybe she hadn't told him that she called me.

Dontae returned, carrying a blanket." I figure we could sit, eat and converse about whatever you going through."

He placed it on the floor and sat the food on top of it. "This is something like an indoor picnic, but you probably think it's lame. I know you like rough-ass niggas. I'm from the hood too, I just move different. Don't forget that."

"I don't think that and I actually enjoy simple things. The gesture is very sweet."

"Good." Dontae grabbed my hand and helped me get onto the floor.

"Now, if I get stuck down here, it's your fault," I joked, while leaning against the sofa in search of a comfortable spot.

"I'm not weak and I can lift all of you. Believe that." He winked and sat down on the blanket. One by one, he pulled out both containers and sat one down in front on me.

"I'm sure you can, if you can kill with your bare hands." The rice bowl from Chipotle was my favorite and he knew just what I liked.

"I kill everything I touch." Dontae held his stare, undressing me with his eyes and I knew he was being nasty, but I didn't say anything. "Well anyway, let's talk about you. What happened now?"

"Why you say it like that?" I was almost defensive, but I had to remember he only had my best interest at heart.

"That's a silly question and you know that. You know how I feel about your situation."

"You're right," I agreed, while placing a scoop of rice into my mouth.

"I know and I'm waiting."

Once I chewed and swallowed my food, I started off with the incident at the mall and my meeting with dear old Crystal. The entire time I talked, Dontae ate his food and shook his head in disapproval from time to time. Each incident I told out loud made me realize how stupid he had me looking in the public's eye. Hell, I felt like a fool repeating the shit and that alone was more than enough to make me see it was time to end things for good.

"Go ahead, because I know you have a lot to say. Just tell me how stupid you think I am for staying with him."

"I'm not going to do that, because I would never call you stupid. You're just not making the best decisions. Being in lust can make you do some crazy shit, such as staying in an unhealthy relationship and that's exactly what you are in." Dontae draped his arm over my shoulder and played with my hair. "You have to know your worth and when you do, you'll stop settling for anything."

"I know, but he wasn't like this in the beginning. He was sweet. I know he loves me, but—"

Dontae cut me off abruptly. "He has a funny way of showing it. Don't take this the wrong way, but if he loved you the way you say he does or did, then no woman would ever have the ability to come to you as a woman. Do you catch my drift?"

"I do."

"If we were together, you would never have to worry about me cheating on you or another woman coming to you about anything." Dontae's eyes were on my face and I could feel him looking deep into my soul. "I would always treat you like a queen because that's what you deserve, and I know that's what your father would want for you."

I had faith in his words, but I wasn't trying to hear broken promises from another man. There was only one that walked planet earth that I trusted a thousand percent and that was Leonard Jordan, my father.

"I hear you." My response was nonchalant, but it wasn't because of him. That has everything to do with Coy.

"Are you done?"

"For now, I am." Dontae picked up our food containers and placed them back into the brown bag. Then he stood to his feet and placed it on the coffee table. "I'll be right back."

Dontae was right, and I couldn't argue with that. I just let everything sink in. Speaking of the devil, my cellphone sang, and I already knew it was Coy by the ringtone alone. When I looked down at the screen, his picture popped up, clouding my thoughts. Coy had two jobs and he couldn't even do that shit right. He was supposed to remain faithful and take care of all my needs, but he failed tremendously. Now, the question was if I knew all of this, why was I broken and confused? The answer was simple. I loved him with every fiber in my body. Coy gave me something no other man had the opportunity to do. My greatest gift, my son. It was sad he was so selfish and didn't know what to do with it. He ruined the chance for us to be a happy family.

Picking up the phone, I clutched it close to my heart with tears in my eyes. I knew if I answered, he would persuade me to come back. Eventually, the phone hung up, but not even twenty seconds later, he was calling right back. The urge to ignore him faded away and I accepted his call and placed it to my ear.

"Hello."

"Where you at? And why you not answering the phone?" Coy was shouting like a maniac in my ear.

"I'm out on a drive. I needed time to think," I replied.

"Think about what, baby?" His tone changed, but that was only a ploy to get me home.

"Why couldn't you just be the person that I fell in love with?" I whispered into the phone. "I trusted you."

"I am. Now what you talking about? You doing all that talking in a circle. Just come out and say it."

My lips started to move, but they stopped when Dontae entered the room. True enough, he knew what was going on, but now things had gotten just a bit more awkward. He looked at me for confirmation, so I nodded my head and put my finger over my lips to keep him from saying anything. The last thing I needed was for Coy to hear another man in the background.

"I know all about the baby with Crystal. Her name is Jayla and she's cute, by the way. She looks just like you. I also know about the female you're supposed to be meeting up with when she gets off work at nine."

My emotions were beginning to run wild, but this time, I had Dontae's shoulder to cry on. "Who the fuck told you that?"

"It doesn't matter who told me. The only thing that matters is if it's true or not. And you can start by confessing at any moment now."

"Lani, baby, just come home so we can sit down and talk about this please. I'm sorry, but I need you here with me," he pleaded.

The tears started to fall once again, but heavier. "Coy, you don't need me. You can have any female you want. I just don't understand that if this was the way you were going to treat me, why didn't you just let me go off to college? Why keep me here just to mistreat me and having me looking stupid?"

"Fuck them other ho's. I don't want them. I love you and that's why I got you pregnant on purpose. If I would've let you leave, you would've forgotten all about me when you got up there with those college dudes."

Those words knocked the wind out of me. *On purpose? Was he serious?* "If that is true, then that was very selfish on your behalf. You knew my father didn't want me to have a baby and you knew that going to college meant everything to me. I can't believe you," I screeched, rubbing the water from my eyes.

"Well believe it and no, I don't regret it," he stated as a matter-of-fact. "Now come home and we can finish this face-to-face."

"No. I'm not coming there."

"You don't have a fuckin' choice."

Dontae looked at me and shook his head no. Then mouthed the words, *tell him.* I couldn't lie, I was a little afraid to tell him it was over. Dontae reached for my phone. I thought he was about to take it, but he put it on speaker, so he could hear exactly what was being said.

"Coy, I'm never coming back."

"You better bring your ass home and I'm not playing wit' cho ass. Get the fuck here now," he screamed into the phone.

"Why do you want me there? So you can hit me again? Look at how you're acting. I can only imagine what you will do if I came there, knowing what I know."

"Bitch!" he shouted. "If you don't come here tonight, I swear to God, when you step foot in here, I'm beating your ass. You think I fucked you up all those other times? Nah. This ass whooping gone be the worst one yet and you can mark my muthafuckin' words. And, I'm gone lock yo' ass up, so you can't go nowhere. A bitch get a l'il leeway and some fresh air and get bold."

Dontae was livid. He snatched the phone from my hand, scratching my hand in the process. "Fuck nigga, I wish you would put your hands on her."

"Yo, who the fuck is this? And why the fuck you on my lady phone?"

"Nigga you know who the fuck this is. We done met before."

"I know this ain't Dontae?"

"You guessed right. Now threaten me. As a matter of fact, fight me, since you so muthafuckin' tough. You don't get cool points for beating on a female and a pregnant one at that."

"Oh, so y'all fuckin' now? Leilani, you gone have to see me and when you do, I'm killing yo' ass. I told you I wasn't lettin' you go. That ass better walk light, 'cause when I catch you, it's lights out. And that goes for you too, fuck boy Roy, while you tryin' to save her."

"You know those empty threats don't mean shit to me. When you see me, don't hesitate to pull that trigger, because I certainly won't."

"Fuck you Leilani. You ain't shit ho'."

Dontae hung up on Coy and tossed my phone onto the couch. My feelings were hurt, but at that point nothing else mattered, because I knew Coy would make good on his promise.

"This nigga been beating on you too? Yo, what the fuck wrong with you?" I ignored him. Coy had already answered that question for him. "Come on, Leilani, you was raised better than that." Dontae was full of anger, because he never spoke to me in an aggressive manner.

"Please don't yell at me. I got that enough on a daily basis with him." I sniffled and covered my face with my hands. "Just talk to me."

Dontae sighed loudly and rubbed his hand over his face. "You right. I'm sorry. I'm just so pissed that you would let this nigga treat you like this. Females that normally end up like this are ones looking for a father figure. You grew up with your father, so I just don't understand it and don't give me that virgin bullshit, because that's no excuse."

The way he was talking to me made me cry harder and he knew it. "Leilani, you deserve much more than what he gave you. In so many words, I've told you I wanted to be with you. The day I saw you in the store, all of my old feelings resurfaced. I've never stopped loving you. When I was in the service, I thought about you every day. If you would've stayed with me, you could've had a good life right now. I just want you to give us a second chance."

Dontae's words were soothing, and it felt good to be genuinely loved by a man other than my father. I knew he was telling the truth, but I searched his deep, brown tantalizing eyes for confirmation anyway.

"Do you really mean that?"

"I can show you that I really mean it." Dontae grabbed the side of my face and stroked it gently. His touch sent chills all over my body. "Words can't express the way I feel about you. Just know I would never treat you like that. If you take this next step with me, I promise you won't regret it."

Coy and I hadn't been broken up a full sixty minutes and I wasn't quite ready to start another relationship. Besides, I had far too much baggage and now I was a target in my baby father's eyes.

"Dontae, that sounds good, but I'm pregnant with another man's child and it's too early for me to jump into another relationship, without closing the door on the last one. I'm just not ready."

"Do you want him out of the picture?"

"I do."

"You can honestly look in my eyes and say that what you had with him is over?"

"Yes. It's over and I'm never going back to him. You heard what he said to me and look at what he did to me." I pulled my bottom lip down so he could see where my teeth broke the skin when Coy hit me.

"That's all I needed to know."

Dontae's hand was still on my tear-stained face, when he leaned in and placed his lips on top of mine. They were soft and cool to the touch, so I kissed him back. As our kiss deepened, our tongues grabbed ahold of each other. The warmth of his frisky hands, elicited a strong desire to go further, as I felt his hand creep underneath my dress and make its way up my thigh. He squeezed them gently and my breath got caught in my throat, but that wasn't enough to make me stop though. Then his hand went further and I could feel his fingertips grazing the seat of my panties. Instantly, I panicked.

"Dontae, wait, I don't think I'm ready for this yet."

"I'll be gentle, I promise."

Dontae moved his lips from mine and placed them in the crook of my neck. His tongue rolled around in circles, before coming to a complete stop to suck on that one spot. My body was growing weak by the millisecond and I tried my best to keep my composure, but he was making that hard to do. I even tried clutching my pearls and locking my legs, but that didn't work either. Dontae was too determined to get between my legs. His

166

fingers maneuvered past my panties, until they found my lips and made their way into my opening. I could feel his finger slide in and out of my wetness, so I closed my eyes and allowed our chemistry to take control. Me sleeping with Dontae wasn't going to make me feel no worse than I already did, and at that moment, I no longer cared. I saved my virginity all those years, only to give it up to someone that didn't give a fuck about me in the end. My body count officially went up to two within days of each other.

"Lay back." Following his instructions, I sat up and laid my fat ass down on the blanket. He grabbed a pillow from the sofa and placed it underneath my head. "Is that comfortable for you?"

"Yeah."

Dontae got on his knees and pulled off my panties, tossing them off to the side. Then he got down lower and kissed my throbbing, thick wet lips with his soft set of lips. He tongue kissed my pussy pearl and penetrated my kitty with his finger at the same time. My hips moved at his rhythm, following his every command.

"Ahh. Ss. Ouu," I moaned and licked my lips. His tenderness and the way he handled my body made me feel so good all over. I didn't know how long he sucked, slurped and fingered my box, but it wasn't long before I started to have a hard, pleasurable orgasm. Dontae sucked every drop I deposited on his tongue.

When he was done, he got on his knees and wiped his mouth with the back on his hand. Kneeling between my legs, he raised one of them and placed it on the couch. Then, he entered my box with his rock-hard wood and stroked me with ease. My lips gripped his thick dick, as he pushed in and out of me with precaution. That was something I didn't get from Coy. Whenever we had sex, he fucked me hard with no regard to the pain he inflicted on me. It felt so good, I had to call his name.

"Dontae. Dontae."

"What's wrong? Am I hurting you?"

"No," I answered truthfully. "It feels good."

"I've dreamed of making love to you and now I have my chance." He held my other leg up and continued to stroke me graciously. "It feels good to me too."

Dontae stayed inside my pussy for a long time and I didn't mind at all. He took his time with me and hit every corner of my walls. Using his thumb, he rubbed my clit and after a while, I came in contact with yet another orgasm. I swore I could feel my walls shake right before it erupted, giving him a creamy shower. We went at it a little while longer, before he finally came inside of me.

"Damn, this the best pussy I ever had," he admitted. "How do you feel?"

"I'm good."

"Come on, let's go in the bedroom." Dontae stood over me and picked me up with no problem and escorted me to his bed.

"Lay down and I'll be right back."

"Where are you going?"

"I need to make an important business call."

"Okay." Patiently, I laid in the middle of the bed, hugging a pillow until he returned.

Dontae had been gone for at least a good thirty minutes before he finally crawled into bed. We laid face-to-face. "Sorry about that, baby, it took longer than expected."

"That's okay. You're here now." I planted a kiss on his lips and closed my eyes.

For the rest of the night, he held me tight in his arms. Dontae made me feel loved and that was what I needed. And definitely something I could get used to. I just hoped he kept his promise and treated me the way he promised.

Chapter 18

Coy

Leilani had me so muthafuckin' mad, I couldn't function properly and I damn sure couldn't stay in the apartment. The shit she pulled with that nigga was grounds for her to die. She really fucked up my night with that bullshit. That ho' had a lot of nerve to be laid up with the next nigga, letting him feed my son. She better watch her back, because when I got ahold of her that would be her last day breathing. I was supposed to meet Whitney when she got off work, but when I got back home, I saw a lot of Leilani's things were missing. Whitney had to wait, so I told her I would call her, something came up.

Since that shit popped off, she hit me up again, letting me know I could come see her. Apparently, her mama was out of town and she wanted me to slide. Before I headed in her direction I stopped by the liquor store to get me some Yak and Magnums. It was a little after midnight, so I hoped she knew she was getting fucked when I got there. I only came out late for two things and that was money or pussy. Anything else was uncivilized.

The streets were dark, but it was some folks hanging out making noise. I had my chrome .45 with me, so I was on point. Whitney lived in Palm Aire, off McNab and 31st Avenue, so when I was close I called her back.

"Hello."

"I'm at the gate, what I press?"

"Star fifty-five sixty."

When I pressed the numbers, I heard a dial tone and then a long beeping noise right before the gate opened. "It's open."

"Go left and come straight back to the building facing you and I'll be standing by the door."

"Yeah."

I hung up the phone and made a quick left, before parking in front of her building. When I hit the lights, I could see a silhouette, so I grabbed my bag and got out the car. Whitney was in front of her apartment door looking edible, wearing only a bathrobe and a devilish grin on her face. My assumptions were correct, because l'il mama knew what time it was. I walked up and kissed her on the cheek.

"If I didn't know any better, I would think you were waiting on me."

"And you would be correct." Whitney winked at me with pure seduction and stood on her tippy toes. "Why else would I tell you my mama's out of town?"

She grabbed my crotch and licked around my earlobe. Oh yeah, Whitney was a hot thot and ready to bust that twat open for a real nigga. I guess it was the few dollars I hit her with to sway her.

"Come on." She grabbed my hand and led me into the apartment. The place wasn't close to what I expected. There were moving boxes scattered across the floor. The shit was so bad, I had to squeeze between the little walkway that was left open.

"Sorry about the mess. We just moved in and haven't unpacked just yet."

"I was hoping y'all were moving out or in, 'cause this too much shit to be walking through on a regular basis."

"You silly." Whitney led me into a plain all-white bedroom that housed a queen sized bed with colorful sheets and pillows. "Don't talk about my room either, because I have to decorate it after the movers drop off the rest of our stuff tomorrow."

"I ain't got shit to say."

"Good. Have a seat and whatever thoughts you do have, keep them to yourself."

She was feisty as fuck. I sat down on the edge of the bed and took out the liquor bottle, cups and ice. "You want a cup?"

"Yeah, fix me one." Whitney stood in front of me smiling and fidgeting with the tie on her robe. "So, where is your baby mama? I'm surprised you came over."

The mention of Leilani made me stop pouring and look up at her with a snarl. "Why you asking about her?"

"I was just curious."

"We ain't together."

"Oh, my bad. I guess that's a touchy subject." She loosened up the tie on her robe. "But, that's fine, I don't wanna talk. I'm ready to fuck."

Her straightforwardness caught me off guard and I damn near dropped my drink. But when she opened the robe and let it fall to the floor, my mouth fell open. She was butt-ass naked. Her yellow skin looked as if it had been kissed by the sun. My eyes zoomed in on her neatly trimmed, plump little pussy. The patch of hair she left was shaped in a perfect rectangle and the same color like the hair on her head. The view was nice and so was the gap between her legs.

Whitney walked slowly towards me until she was standing close enough for me to smell the scent of whatever soap she bathed with and took the drink from my hand. I watched closely as she put it to her mouth and gulped it down.

"Fix me another one." She handed the cup back to me and I refilled it for her. "Drink up," she smiled.

"I'm on ya' ass, don't worry." I fixed myself a double shot of yack and downed that bitch. It was time to strap up. "Back up."

I stood up and removed my clothing piece by piece and tossed them on the floor. It wasn't like she had some place for me to put my shit. "Get up on the bed."

"Hold on, let me put on some music."

"Nah, your moans gon' be good enough for me. Now get up on the bed and lay on your stomach." I grabbed the pack of condoms from the bed, took one out and opened it.

"You sound confident." She crawled up on the bed and laid down the way I told her to.

Once I put the condom on, I was ready to pound some shit. I grabbed her by the waist and pulled that ass back to me. "Toot that ass in the air."

Whitney arched her back, giving me full access to the pussy. That thang was sitting pretty from the back. I sunk in deep and she howled, and leaned forward with her head down.

"That's why I'm confident." That made me smirk, because I hadn't even started to beat the pussy up. "You running from the dick already."

Slowly, I pulled out and rammed it back in and she screamed. "Ouch!" She looked back at me. "You doing that on purpose."

"Un-huh." I pulled out again and rammed my dick back inside. After teasing her for a little bit, I relentlessly pumped in and out the twat. Her pussy wasn't better than Leilani's and her shit wasn't hella tight either. So, that led me to believe she had a lot of bodies underneath her belt, whenever her mama wasn't home.

"Ooh, yeah. Do it harder," she moaned with great aggression, while gripping the sheets and throwing it back like a pro. Whitney got a little wild when I smacked her on the ass.

"Pull my hair," she demanded.

That made a nigga smile, because she liked that rough shit and I was with that. I grabbed her short curly and pulled it hard, snatching her head back while I punished the pussy. A nigga could get used to this, especially since Crystal done blew up a nigga spot. I already knew it was her that told Leilani about the baby since no one knew about her. It was cool though, because I had a fresh ass whooping for that ho' too. When I was finished with her, she would be slurping pizza from a straw.

"Fuck me back."

I stood still behind Whitney and let her do the work. For her to have a small booty, that muthafucka moved like waves in the ocean. She definitely knew how to fuck. Her pussy was sucking my dick so good, I felt like doing the Dougie while I was back there chillin' and enjoying the view. Whitney's pussy started to spit some white creamy shit all over the condom. She slammed her ass hard against my pelvis.

"Get on top," she moaned.

Whitney stopped and eased up to the head of the bed and I followed. When I got on top, I put my dick back in and pounded in and out. I put both of her legs on my shoulders and went ham in the pussy. She was very flexible, but that dick hurt when it was in that stomach.

"Oooh yeah. Fuck this pussy." Her eyes were closed and the sound of her voice and fuck faces were turning me on. My thrusts were long and strong. I was trying to break a bone while I was in it.

"You look so good taking this dick." Whitney put her hand between her legs and rubbed her clit.

"Move your hand so I can see that pussy. I'ma make you cum all over this dick."

"Ouu, yes baby. This big ass dick feel so good."

"Yeah."

"Fuck yeah. Now I see why your baby mama was mad at you."

She just had to bring her up in the conversation once again. So, to keep her quiet, I pinned her legs all the way back to the wall and beat the brakes and gas line out that pussy. From there, all I heard was moaning and constant screaming. That sounded a lot better than her stupid ass comments.

"Oh my God. Fuck. Fuck. Fuck," she hollered.

I could feel myself on the verge of catching a nut. The pressure was so intense that I could feel it in my stomach. I was ready for it too because after I caught it, my ass was going home. The sudden click from behind was a sound I knew all too well and I froze after. Whitney stopped moaning and grabbed the sheet in an effort to cover herself up, so I released her legs.

"What the fuck you in here doing fucking this nigga?" a deep voice boomed from behind me.

"Why do you have a gun, stupid?" Whitney snapped. "And, why you in my room?"

That shit was blowing me, so I turned to look behind me. Just as I made eye contact with the nigga holding the gun, he hit me over the head with it. I was dizzy as fuck when my body crashed against the mattress.

"Shut yo' ass up, 'cause you the stupid one. Did this nigga pay you? You said he had money."

"You could've let me get a nut first. Damn. You always fucking up shit," Whitney angrily shouted.

I grabbed my head and I could feel the warm blood trickling down the side of my face. "You know this nigga?"

"Yeah. That's my brother."

"Bitch, you set me up?" I spat, pissed as fuck because I let my dick get me jammed up in some bullshit.

"No, I didn't. His ass not even supposed to be here."

Whitney got up from the bed and put her robe back on. For somebody that had nothing to do with this shit, her ass was mighty calm. Her brother walked to the bed and hit me again, but that time it was in the face.

"Don't call my sister no bitch, homie." He looked back at her. "Check that nigga pockets."

Blood was in my eyes, but I could see her bend down and grab my pants. All the money I had from earlier that day was still in there, so they made a few easy bands off my ass. When I got out the car, I was fasting and left my gun under the seat. Now I was fucked.

"Nigga get up and put your clothes on and for the record, I'm doing this for your baby mama. Whitney, back up so he don't try no slick shit." Her brother had his piece aimed at me.

"My baby mama?" Now I was confused.

"That's what I said," he snapped back.

When I sat up and scooted across the bed I felt dizzy as fuck. Even if I could take the gun, I couldn't see worth a damn, so fighting back was useless. It took me a few minutes to get fully dressed, but once I had on everything, I sat down on the bed. My head was throbbing like a muthafucka.

"Get the nigga cellphone, so he can call Leilani."

When I heard him say that, I ignored the pain and sized him up, because if he thought he was about to do anything to her, he was sadly mistaken.

"How you know my lady, nigga?" I spat.

"Pipe that shit down. You ain't running shit right now, I am." He waved the gun in my direction. "You gone call her and apologize for all the shit you put her through. Tell her you love her."

"I'm not doing that. Fuck outta here with that fuck shit."

"Bruh, you out of options. You can tell her you sorry and try to make shit right before you die. Or you can die with guilt on your heart. Either way, you are going to die."

"A'ight. I'll do it." Due to my slip-up, I didn't have a choice. Whitney handed me the phone and I dialed her number. All it did was ring constantly. "She not answering."

"Call it again," her brother demanded.

When I called back that time, she picked up. "Why are you calling me, Coy?" Her voice was groggy.

"I want to apologize for everything I did to you. The abuse, cheating and lies. I'm sorry. You deserve more than I ever gave you and I hope you can find it in your heart to forgive me. No matter what happens, just know that I love you from the bottom of my heart. Don't ever forget that and please take care of my son. Tell him about me and that I was happy he was coming into the world. Let him know that I'm sorry I won't be here when he's born. I left you something in the secret spot and the code is the date that we met. Find your happiness and I love you until I take my last breath."

"Coy, what's wrong?" The tone of her voice was filled with a great deal of panic.

"Just know that I've loved you since the day we met as kids and it has always been my mission to make you mine when I got older."

"Coy, what are you talking about?"

"We met at my dad's house. He used to live in the same neighborhood, before there was a home invasion and he was killed. When I got away, I fled and changed my name when I turned eighteen."

"Oh my God." She was hyperventilating on the phone. "You're Josiah?"

Just as I was about to respond, Whitney's brother snatched the phone and hung it up. "Why did you do that?"

"You made your peace and now it's time to go." Her brother looked me in the eyes and pulled the trigger twice, hitting me in the chest. My body flew backwards on the bed. Staring up at the ceiling, my eyes rolled to the back of my head and I closed my eyes.

Chapter 19

Leilani

The call I had just received me from Coy had me shook. Frantically, I called him right back. My heart was pounding furiously out my chest and my mind was in a frenzy. No matter what he had done to me, I couldn't fathom something terrible happening to him because at the end of the day, he was still the father of my son. After his phone went to voicemail, I called him back. This time it went straight to voicemail and I panicked, darting back into the room.

"Dontae, wake up. Dontae." He was like a sleeping giant. I pushed and shook him, until he finally opened his eyes.

"What's wrong, baby?"

"I don't know. I just got a call from Coy."

Dontae jumped up from the bed with his face balled up. "Did he threaten you again? Because if he did, I'm going to find his ass right now."

"No. No. That's not it. Something is wrong." I sat down on the bed and rubbed my temple in confusion. "He called to apologize about everything he did to me."

"As he should."

"But, that's not it. He told me to take care of the baby and to make sure he knows about him. I'm telling you something is wrong. It almost..." The idea that surfaced in my mind caused me to freeze for a moment. "It's like he's about die. Like commit suicide or something. I need to find him."

"Why do you want to find him? That could be a trap to get you back over there. Don't fall for that, Leilani. You're too smart for that."

"I know, but I don't think that's the case." None of it was making sense, but Dontae did have a point. What if it was all a part of his plan to get me home, so he could kill me? My mind and heart needed to get on one accord because I was going crazy with the back and forth.

Dontae sat beside me and took my hand into his, then looked into my eyes. "Baby, let's just go back to bed. It's not safe for you to go over there."

"Alright. I get it."

Sleep did not come for me at all, because my mind wouldn't let me rest. So, I just stared at the walls in complete darkness, until I heard Dontae snoring like a baby bear. Cautiously, I slipped from underneath him, threw on my clothes and grabbed my phone, just in case he called back. Whatever my fate was, was going to be in the hands of the Lord, because I was going to make sure he was okay. If I had to apologize and beg for his forgiveness for hurting him by allowing Dontae to talk to him in that manner, then that's what I was prepared to do.

As I tip toed from the room, I crept down the hallway, grabbed my keys and slipped out the door. The elevator wasn't too far away, but I had to move quick as I could, just in case he woke up looking for me. I knew he would be upset, but I would deal with him later.

The sun was on the verge of rising when I made it outside in the parking lot and into my car. Normally, I didn't drive fast, but since this was an emergency, I put the pedal to the metal and hauled ass.

It took me twenty minutes to get to the apartment and when I got there, Coy's car wasn't in the parking lot. That was a clear sign that he wasn't home, but I wanted to go inside and check anyway. When I got upstairs, I unlocked the door and went inside. The apartment was the same exact way that I left it. From what I could see at first glance, nothing was out of place.

"Coy."

I called out just in case he was in the bedroom to avoid a blitz attack. As I walked into the room, the bed was still intact, so I knew he hadn't slept there. A bad feeling came over me, so I sat down on the bed and dialed his number once again. It rang a few times before it went to the voicemail. That time, I left a message.

"Coy, please call me. I'm so worried about you. I love you and I'm sorry. Just call me back and let me know you're okay."

After I hung up, I went to the closet to see what he left for me. Buried behind a pile of clothes was a safe, knee-high tall. I put in the numbers of the day we met and the door came ajar. Inside the safe were neat stacks of bills, filled almost to the top. Tears built up in my eyes and slid down my cheeks. There was a black satin box sitting in the front of the safe and when I opened it, I grew more emotional than I had been. It was a diamond ring.

"He was going to propose to me?" I took the ring out the box and stared at in admiration. After all the shit he put me through, I guess he changed his mind about asking me to marry him. The sound of my cellphone made my heart skip a beat, so I stopped what I was doing and ran to get my phone. Coy was calling me back and I had to admit, I was happy about it.

"Baby, where are you? I'm home, looking for you," I babbled on and on.

"Ma'am, slow down." A guy said, ruining my thoughts.

"Who is this?"

"This is the Broward County's Sheriff's Office. Who is this?"

"Leilani. Where is Coy? Is he in jail?"

"What's your relationship with him?" he asked.

"I'm his girlfriend."

"Okay, well, we need you to come down to the station."

"For what?"

"I can't disclose that information on the phone. Come down to the Public Safety Building on 27th Avenue and ask for Detective Mills."

"Okay. I'm on my way."

I hung up the phone and went back inside the closet to close the safe and cover it back up with the clothes that kept it hidden. "He better not be in no shit," I mumbled.

***

After I checked in and received my visitor's pass, I was escorted to a back office to wait on Detective Mills. Dontae was calling, but I didn't answer. The interrogation room is where they had me seated, so that confused me. I was familiar with the room from watching crime shows and I didn't know anything about his business, so I was hoping that wasn't why they called me down. A few minutes later the door opened and a light-skinned black man walked in, wearing black slacks and a white collared shirt.

"Leilani Jordan?" He scoped me out from head to toe, but instantly came back to my belly.

"Yes."

"Your father is Leonardo Jordan?"

"Yes."

"Oh, wow. He's a really good friend of mine, but I haven't seen you in a while."

"I remember you." He did look familiar when he walked in, but I wasn't too sure.

Detective Mills sat down at the table and slid a plastic bag across the table, along with his cellphone. I noticed right away that it was Coy's wallet and car keys inside the bag. "What did he do?"

"Leilani, I'm so sorry and I don't know how to tell you this. But this morning, we found Coy in his vehicle with two gunshots to the chest."

"No. No," I screamed loud enough for the entire building to hear me. That was the last thing I thought he was going to say. I would've preferred it if he said he robbed someone instead. Any news would've been better than what he had just told me.

*　*　*

Dontae

Leilani was nowhere to be found when I got up and when I called her, she didn't answer the phone. I didn't know where she went, but I knew she was okay. I figured that she needed a little time to herself, so I took that as an opportunity to handle my business. Thirty minutes passed, as I sat patiently in the shopping plaza on 31st Avenue, outside of the restaurant, Pleasure of the Sea. I ordered me some fish and shrimp while I waited on my cousins to pull up.

Just as I finished scoffing down the last of my French fries, a black Cadillac CTS pulled up and they both got out smiling. Whitney climbed in the back and Jamison hopped in the front.

"What it do, cuzzo?" He tried dapping me up, but I gave him my elbow since my fingers were greasy.

"Waiting on y'all slow asses." I sat the plastic bag on the floor and wiped my hands with a wet nap. "So, how that shit went last night?"

"Well, you know Thotianna fucked the nigga, of course."

Whitney slapped him in the back of the head. "Shut up and stop worrying about who I fuck. I don't be worried about who sister you stick your dick in."

"Other than that, the shit went smooth. I made that nigga call Leilani and apologize before I killed him. At least that will help her cope a little more, knowing he didn't die mad at her."

"Grab the envelope in the glovebox. It's ten bands, y'all split that shit down the middle, and thanks for handling that nigga for me."

"You know it's all good, cuz." Jamison opened the glovebox and thumbed through the bills.

"It's all there," I replied.

"I know it is."

"Hold up, it's her calling me back." I grabbed my phone and slid the green icon. "What's up, baby?"

"He's dead. He's dead," Leilani cried. "Somebody killed him. He didn't commit suicide."

"Damn, baby, I'm sorry to hear that. Where are you?"

Leilani let out a loud scream and I could hear someone in the background telling her to breathe. "Ahh. It hurts. I can't do this by myself."

"Baby, what's wrong?" She didn't answer me.

"Hello." It was a man.

"Who is this?" I asked out of curiosity.

"This is Detective Mills. Leilani's water broke and the paramedics are about to take her to the hospital."

"Which one?"

"Plantation General, so meet her there."

"I'm on my way." I hung up the phone. "I gotta bounce, she's in labor. I'll hit y'all up later."

"A'ight, fam."

***

On my way to the hospital, I caught a flashback of last night's events. After Leilani told me about the incident at the mall and the female he was trying to holla at, it sounded just like my cousin, Whitney. So, when we went to bed and I told her that I had an important call to make, I hit up Whitney. She confirmed she met a dude named Coy and he was supposed to come see her. Immediately, I put the plan into play and called her brother, Jamison, since he's a cop. I explained that Coy was abusive and threatened to kill her and me when he found out she left him. He promised to handle it, so I threw in a bonus for his trouble.

Coy deserved to die because of the way he treated Leilani, because she didn't deserve that. And, now that he was out the way, I got my lady back. That situation made me feel like less of a man when I wasn't helping her, which was why I asked her if she wanted him out the picture. So of course, I didn't feel bad for the way things went down. I knew he would kill me or Leilani, if he had the opportunity, so I beat him to it.

When I made it to the hospital, I rushed to the Labor and Delivery ward. I ran down the hallway in search of her to make sure I didn't miss the birth of my step-son. I loved Leilani with every breath in my body. She was a nigga rib and the reason why I continued to breathe. After we got over this roadblock, I had plans on asking her to marry me. There was no point in waiting when you found your one true love and Leilani was just that to me.

By the time I made it to the room, I saw that she wasn't alone and that was a surprise in itself. It had been so long since we saw one another, but he smiled when he saw me. I walked up and shook his hand and he gave me a hug.

"It's good to see you. What brought you by?" Mr. Jordan asked.

"Well, I moved back in town a few months ago and ran into your daughter. Since then, we remained in contact. You know I still love her."

"I know you do, son. Did you get married while you was away?" he asked, with a huge grin on his face.

"Nah." I leaned in and whispered in his ear so that Leilani couldn't hear me. "Hopefully, I get to marry her."

"Hmm." He stroked his chin. "We'll see about that. I want you to come by, so we can have dinner and catch up."

"I'm surprised to see you here, with everything y'all been through." I wanted to see where his head was at.

"A friend of mine called and told me what happened. I love my daughter and I'm still mad at her, but she needs me more than ever now."

"I'm so glad to hear that. She was really torn up about it and I had to put that nigga in check myself about her."

"Ughhhh. Get this thing out of me," Leilani shouted.

"Let me get over here and calm her down. We'll talk later," I said with a smile.

"Good luck. I done tried." He sat down in the chair that was up against the wall.

"Baby, just relax." I leaned down and kissed her face. "I'm here for you and it's going to be okay."

"That's easy for you to say, because you not the one having contractions."

"You right. Hold my hand." Leilani grabbed ahold of my hand and damn near broke off every finger. "Damn, you strong, girl."

After all that yelling and screaming for an hour, Leilani finally gave birth to a beautiful, bouncing baby boy and I could see the joy in her eyes when she met her prince for the first time. Never in my life had I witnessed something so beautiful, yet gross in my life. The service didn't have shit on that childbirth experience. I couldn't wait until the day she had my child, but that would be a long time from now. Until then, I'll just take on my new responsibility.

Epilogue

18 months later

The past year of my life had been hell, to say the least. After Coy's funeral, I fell into a terrible depression and even contemplated committing suicide on more than one occasion. Just the sight of my son on a daily basis triggered every raw emotion in my body and it was hard to deal with it, because he looked so much like his father. Then, on top of all of that, they never solved his murder, so they labeled it a cold case after six months. That made things worse, because I never got closure and Coy didn't get justice.

Despite all things, I had a solid foundation of help with everything I faced. Dontae was amazing. He easily stepped up and played the father role in my son's life, and I was grateful for him every day. He even made sure I received the best counseling to help with my depression. He was my real-life angel, because he came in the nick of time to heal my broken heart. Dontae showed me real love. Things that Coy never showed me. He didn't raise his voice at me and he never, ever put his hands on me. We weren't perfect, but we were close.

Then, there was my father, he came back into my life and played an active role in my son's life as well. A month after the baby was born, we all sat down at the dinner table and hashed out our differences. I could honestly say I was in a good place and it felt good.

As I sat underneath the tree, I smiled while watching my father and husband, play ball with DJ. After spending the third day in the hospital with no name for my son, I decided to name him after Dontae, since he was going to be the one to raise him. Of course that was my father's idea and he was very persuasive about it. Eventually, marriage followed, so I was good with the name.

My family walked in my direction, so I stood up and met them halfway.

"Did my men have fun playing?"

"I did, I did, Mommy." I kneeled down and picked him up.

"I'm too old for this shit." My father laughed, while holding his back. "We have to get on the road if we want to beat this crazy traffic."

"I'm not ready for y'all to go." I squeezed my baby in my arms and kissed his face. "I love you so much and I'm going to miss you. Be good for Daddy, Nana and Papa, okay?"

"Okay."

It was hard to let him go, but if I wanted to secure my son's future, I knew what had to be done.

"It's okay, baby, we'll FaceTime you every day." I handed the baby to Dontae and gave him a kiss.

"I'm going to miss you too."

"Y'all gone be okay." My father stepped in between us and stole a hug.

"I love you, Daddy."

"I love you too," he replied.

"Did I miss the farewell?" My mother walked up and stood in front of me.

"Of course, you didn't." Diane embraced me long and hard and I had to admit, it felt good. I couldn't remember the last time she did that before the hatred towards me started.

"I love you so much, Leilani, and I'm sorry for all the bad things I did and said to you." When she looked at me she had tears in her eyes, so I wiped them with my fingers.

"I forgave you already, Mommy, and I love you too. I'm just happy to have you here with me on my special day."

"I'm so proud of you. You're a strong woman and I applaud you for not giving up on your dreams. I mean that." Now she had me teary-eyed. In return, she wiped mine. "Now don't you start crying."

"I'm trying not to."

"Alright, crybabies, let's go," my father shouted. "Leilani, be good and stay focused. We'll see you soon."

"Okay, I love y'all."

Dontae and I hugged and kissed one last time before they walked off, leaving me behind to succeed. I turned around and walked towards the building.

"Is that my bestie bitch walking up here?" Caussia screamed loudly.

"It's me, bitch."

"I'm so happy you finally joining a real girl at Harvard. I see the reunion finally over." She was killing herself laughing.

"Yes, girl."

"Well, let's go inside so I can introduce you to everybody."

"Let's go." I smiled.

Dontae played a huge role in my decision on finally going to Harvard to study law. He took a civilian job to raise our son while I was away, with the help of my parents. My son was in good hands and after I graduated in four years, we were going to be living the life that I'd always dreamed of.

The End

Submission Guideline.

Submit the first three chapters of your completed manuscript to ldpsubmissions@gmail.com, subject line: Your book's title. The manuscript must be in a .doc file and sent as an attachment. Document should be in Times New Roman, double spaced and in size 12 font. Also, provide your synopsis and full contact information. If sending multiple submissions, they must each be in a separate email.

Have a story but no way to send it electronically? You can still submit to LDP/Ca$h Presents. Send in the first three chapters, written or typed, of your completed manuscript to:

LDP: Submissions Dept
Po Box 870494
Mesquite, Tx 75187

DO NOT send original manuscript. Must be a duplicate.

Provide your synopsis and a cover letter containing your full contact information.

Thanks for considering LDP and Ca$h Presents.

Blinded by his Love

Coming Soon from Lock Down Publications/Ca$h Presents

BOW DOWN TO MY GANGSTA

By **Ca$h**

TORN BETWEEN TWO

By **Coffee**

BLOOD STAINS OF A SHOTTA **III**

By **Jamaica**

STEADY MOBBIN II

By **Marcellus Allen**

BLOOD OF A BOSS **V**

By **Askari**

LOYAL TO THE GAME **IV**

By **T.J. & Jelissa**

A DOPEBOY'S PRAYER **II**

By **Eddie "Wolf" Lee**

IF LOVING YOU IS WRONG... **III**

LOVE ME EVEN WHEN IT HURTS

By **Jelissa**

TRUE SAVAGE **V**

By **Chris Green**

BLAST FOR ME **III**

ROTTEN TO THE CORE **III**

By **Ghost**

ADDICTIED TO THE DRAMA **III**

By **Jamila Mathis**

LIPSTICK KILLAH **III**

CRIME OF PASSION **II**

By **Mimi**

WHAT BAD BITCHES DO **III**

By **Aryanna**

THE COST OF LOYALTY **II**

By **Kweli**

SHE FELL IN LOVE WITH A REAL ONE **II**

By **Tamara Butler**

LOVE SHOULDN'T HURT **III**

By **Meesha**

CORRUPTED BY A GANGSTA **III**

By **Destiny Skai**

A GANGSTER'S CODE III

By **J-Blunt**

KING OF NEW YORK II

By **T.J. Edwards**

CUM FOR ME **IV**

By **Ca$h & Company**

WHO SHOT YA II

Renta

<u>Available Now</u>

<u>RESTRAINING ORDER **I & II**</u>

By **CA$H & Coffee**

<u>LOVE KNOWS NO BOUNDARIES **I II & III**</u>

By **Coffee**

<u>RAISED AS A GOON I, II, III & IV</u>

<u>BRED BY THE SLUMS I, II, III</u>

<u>BLAST FOR ME I & II</u>

<u>ROTTEN TO THE CORE I II</u>

Blinded by his Love

CUM FOR ME

CUM FOR ME 2

CUM FOR ME 3

An **LDP Erotica Collaboration**

BRIDE OF A HUSTLA **I II & II**

THE FETTI GIRLS **I, II& III**

CORRUPTED BY A GANGSTA I & II

BLINDED BY HIS LOVE

By **Destiny Skai**

WHEN A GOOD GIRL GOES BAD

By **Adrienne**

A GANGSTER'S REVENGE **I II III & IV**

THE BOSS MAN'S DAUGHTERS

THE BOSS MAN'S DAUGHTERS II

THE BOSSMAN'S DAUGHTERS III

THE BOSSMAN'S DAUGHTERS IV

THE BOSS MAN'S DAUGHTERS **V**

A SAVAGE LOVE **I & II**

BAE BELONGS TO ME

A HUSTLER'S DECEIT I, II

WHAT BAD BITCHES DO I, II

By **Aryanna**

A KINGPIN'S AMBITON

A KINGPIN'S AMBITION **II**

I MURDER FOR THE DOUGH

By **Ambitious**

TRUE SAVAGE

TRUE SAVAGE II

TRUE SAVAGE **III**

Blinded by his Love

TRUE SAVAGE **IV**

By **Chris Green**

A DOPEBOY'S PRAYER

By **Eddie "Wolf" Lee**

THE KING CARTEL **I, II & III**

By **Frank Gresham**

THESE NIGGAS AIN'T LOYAL **I, II & III**

By **Nikki Tee**

GANGSTA SHYT **I II &III**

By **CATO**

THE ULTIMATE BETRAYAL

By **Phoenix**

BOSS'N UP **I , II & III**

By **Royal Nicole**

I LOVE YOU TO DEATH

By Destiny J

I RIDE FOR MY HITTA

I STILL RIDE FOR MY HITTA

By **Misty Holt**

LOVE & CHASIN' PAPER

By **Qay Crockett**

TO DIE IN VAIN

By **ASAD**

BROOKLYN HUSTLAZ

By **Boogsy Morina**

BROOKLYN ON LOCK I & II

By **Sonovia**

GANGSTA CITY

By **Teddy Duke**

Destiny Skai

A DRUG KING AND HIS DIAMOND I & II III

A DOPEMAN'S RICHES

By Nicole Goosby

TRAPHOUSE KING I II & III

By **Hood Rich**

LIPSTICK KILLAH **I, II**

CRIME OF PASSION

By **Mimi**

STEADY MOBBN'

By **Marcellus Allen**

WHO SHOT YA

Renta

<u>BOOKS BY LDP'S CEO, CA$H</u>

<u>TRUST IN NO MAN</u>

<u>TRUST IN NO MAN 2</u>

<u>TRUST IN NO MAN 3</u>

<u>BONDED BY BLOOD</u>

<u>SHORTY GOT A THUG</u>

<u>THUGS CRY</u>

<u>THUGS CRY 2</u>

<u>THUGS CRY 3</u>

<u>TRUST NO BITCH</u>

<u>TRUST NO BITCH 2</u>

<u>TRUST NO BITCH 3</u>

<u>TIL MY CASKET DROPS</u>

<u>RESTRAINING ORDER</u>

<u>RESTRAINING ORDER 2</u>

<u>IN LOVE WITH A CONVICT</u>

<u>Coming Soon</u>

BONDED BY BLOOD 2

BOW DOWN TO MY GANGSTA

CPSIA information can be obtained
at www.ICGtesting.com
Printed in the USA
LVHW011926080721
692196LV00012B/1504